Stranger
From The Stars

Other Avon Camelot Books by
Nancy Etchemendy

THE WATCHERS OF SPACE

NANCY ETCHEMENDY was born and raised in Reno, Nevada. Many of her poems have appeared in small literary magazines. She and her husband now live in Princeton, New Jersey.

Stranger From The Stars

Nancy Etchemendy

Illustrated by Teje Etchemendy

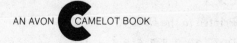

AN AVON CAMELOT BOOK

STRANGER FROM THE STARS is an original publication of Avon Books. This work has never before appeared in book form.

AVON BOOKS
A division of
The Hearst Corporation
959 Eighth Avenue
New York, New York 10019

Book design by Sheldon Winicour
Text Copyright © 1983 by Nancy Etchemendy
Illustrations Copyright © 1983 by Avon Books
Published by arrangement with the author
Library of Congress Catalog Card Number: 83-6022
ISBN: 0-380-83568-1

Library of Congress Cataloging in Publication Data

Etchemendy, Nancy.
  Stranger from the stars.

  (An Avon/Camelot book)
  Summary: Fourteen-year-old Ruthie rescues
Rowen, an old man from the planet Seldor who
has come to earth to study humans, when she finds
him near death after his spaceship has crashed in
the desert.
  [1. Extraterrestrial beings—Fiction.
2. Science fiction] I. Etchemendy, Teje, ill.
II. Title
PZ7.E84St   1983   [Fic]   83-6022
ISBN 0-380-83568-1

First Camelot Printing, June, 1983

CAMELOT TRADEMARK REG. U. S. PAT. OFF. AND IN
OTHER COUNTRIES, MARCA REGISTRADA, HECHO EN
U. S. A.

Printed in the U. S. A.

DON   10 9 8 7 6 5 4 3 2 1

For
John and Crystal

* * * *

With special thanks to
Jon R. Barwise, Hilary Weingarten,
and
Mr. Howell's fifth grade class, 1980–81
Alice Maxwell School,
Sparks, Nevada

TABLE OF CONTENTS

ONE

* * * *

Mystery at
Hidden Creek

RUTHIE crouched behind the massive trunk of a
cottonwood tree and watched the odd-looking
stranger warily, her heart thumping with excitement.
He was no ordinary desert drifter—of that much she
was certain. In fact, he was like no one she'd ever seen
before.

She'd known a few hermits and prospectors, but none
of them looked like the old man in the clearing before
her. For one thing, he had no beard. And his hair, a thin
white fringe above his small ears, was carefully trimmed
and combed. That was unheard of among the drifters who
wandered in from the sagebrush to loiter on the main
street of Sand Fork. They wore their dungarees and
soiled hats like a strange uniform, their hair straggly as
hay and their beards yellow with tobacco juice.

No, this one was disconcertingly different. He wore
a sort of robe. It covered him from the neck to the an-
kles, reminding Ruthie of pictures in a book she had

read about the ancient Greeks. The robe was done in several different colors that seemed to sparkle in the early morning sun. Ruthie wanted to touch it, for she could hardly believe that it was real.

Several hundred feet out in the clearing stood the familiar old miner's shack where she and her friend Kate McGee had spent many pleasant afternoons exploring. It was a natural place to stop, and Ruthie often rested there, even on days like today, when she was alone on a long horseback ride. Hidden Creek ran just a few yards away, its banks sloping gently. Her horse, Sundust, could drink easily here.

But now all of this seemed changed. Hidden Creek Canyon was suddenly exciting in a way it never had been before—magical, and more than a little bit frightening. For today the miner's shack was no longer abandoned. It looked as if this odd stranger had set up housekeeping in the run-down old shanty.

She watched him, hardly daring to breathe. He was making an extraordinary noise—something between a hum and a whistle—as he bustled down to the creek carrying a peculiar container about the size of a bucket. Ruthie observed him with great curiosity as he filled the container and lugged it back up the bank until he came to an open spot where the earth had been freshly turned. Still humming, he poured the water onto the ground carefully.

Ruthie wondered if he might be planting a garden. But that theory didn't quite make sense. She knew far more about growing things than she did about desert men, and she could tell right away that if this was supposed to be a garden, it was not going to amount to much. The dirt was mostly adobe clay and rocks, and if there were rows she certainly couldn't see them.

The old man stood up straight and mopped his wrinkled, reddish forehead with a bright piece of cloth the wrong shape for a bandana. He stopped humming. Slowly, he turned in Ruthie's direction. He opened his mouth, and a sound came out—an eerie whistle that instantly riveted her with terror. She had never heard a human being make any sound like that before. She wanted to run, but her knees felt like gelatin and her feet were suddenly leaden.

The stranger opened his mouth once more. This time, words came out in a silken but weirdly distorted voice. "Good day. I hear you. Please let me see you."

Ruthie felt as if she were trapped in a closet full of rising water. She was *positive* that he couldn't see her. She'd been absolutely silent. She was good at silence, so good that she could sneak to within ten feet of a deer if the wind was right. How could he possibly have heard her?

The thought of stepping out into full view made her break into a cold sweat. Suppose he had a gun! He might shoot her point-blank where she stood. Weirder things than that had happened in the isolated canyons of the desert.

In the midst of this thought, some primitive survival instinct seemed at last to take control of her, and Ruthie found herself dashing like a terrified rabbit through the cottonwoods. She ran straight for Sundust. Leaping into his saddle without ever touching the stirrups, she made him gallop until the shack and the stranger and Hidden Creek Canyon were miles behind. And though she didn't hear any gunshots, she kept her head tucked low until she was sure she was well out of range.

* * *

When she got home, Ruthie ate lunch, then went to her upstairs bedroom and sat down at her desk. The desk, as usual, was covered with bits of wire, drops of solder, and brightly colored electronic components. Ruthie liked fixing up junk radios and televisions, sometimes modifying them for special purposes. Right now, she was trying to build a primitive computer out of old radio parts, light bulbs, and an antique telegraph key that her brother had given her for her birthday. Today, though, her mind kept wandering back to the stranger at Hidden Creek. Electronics seemed boring by comparison. Finally, unable to sit still any longer, Ruthie asked her father if she could go with him to help inspect the fences on the north property line.

"Sure," he said, with a trace of a smile, and motioned her into the back of the jeep.

As they jostled along, she tried at first to join in the small talk with him and their young ranch hand, Tom Castor. She commented on the weather and the grazing and the condition of the new calves. But before long she grew silent. All she could think about was the incident at Hidden Creek. She was still keyed up about it, and thoroughly confused besides. Try as she might, she couldn't make up her mind about whether or not to keep the peculiar old man a secret. The more she thought it over, the more it seemed that her fears had been groundless. He hadn't really done anything that should have been so frightening. Exactly what was it that had scared her so much? In fact, she couldn't say.

They stopped in the shade of a juniper tree. She couldn't help smiling as she watched her father use his teeth to tighten the buckle on the back of his leather glove while he lifted the toolbox from the back of the jeep with his other hand. He was so proud, so independent and capable. If only she could grow up to be all those things herself!

"Tom, you and Ruthie walk on down the property line. Yell if you find any gaps," he said brusquely. "I wanna tighten this section here, then I'll catch up."

Tom and Ruthie had walked for some distance when she heard a strange snorting and the sound of an animal pawing the ground.

"What's that?" she asked, squinting at something that seemed to be moving at a point further up the fence.

"I dunno," said Tom, quickening his pace. "But I think we ought to find out."

Ruthie hesitated a moment before following him. He was barely fourteen—just two years older than she was. Though he was self-confident and even a little cocky, he was still pretty inexperienced about handling stock. If the animal on the fence were a frightened steer, it could be dangerous.

But it wasn't a steer at all. As they approached, Tom exclaimed, "It's an elk, a big one!" He broke into a run.

Ruthie was panting by the time they reached the magnificent animal, its huge rack of antlers caught in the barbed wire.

"I've never seen one so close before," she breathed in amazement. "He's beautiful!"

"He sure is," said Tom. "Look at that rack!"

"What'll we do?" said Ruthie. "How'll we ever get him untangled?"

"That'd be pretty tough." Tom scratched the back of his neck with a freckled hand. "I know what everybody'd say we *ought* to do. We ought to shoot him."

14

"Tom, you wouldn't!" Ruthie was horrified at the thought.

He stood back, crossing his arms and glancing at her disdainfully. " 'Course I would, if I had my rifle. Maybe I'll go back to the jeep and get it."

The elk stopped struggling for a moment, its flanks heaving with exhaustion, its dark eyes rolling with fright.

Tom turned his head away. "Then again, it ain't elk season," he muttered.

"Oh, cut him loose, please!" Ruthie begged, watching in dismay as the animal jerked against the wire, twisting wildly.

"Your pa would have a fit, Ruthie. He'd have to replace the whole section."

"I don't care! Just set it free!" she cried.

Tom squinted in the direction of the jeep. Mr. Keag was a tiny figure in the distance. "Well, okay. But stand back. You never know what a scared animal will do," he said at last, taking a pair of wire cutters from his back pocket.

Holding the cutters at arm's length, Tom severed the wire with a loud crack. The elk, finding itself suddenly free, raised its head and wheeled about, dashing away across the field.

Tom pushed his hat back and wiped his sweating forehead on his shirt sleeve.

Ruthie noticed that his face was pale and his hand shook a little as he slipped the wire cutters back into his pocket. "Kind of scary, huh?" she said, feeling shaky herself.

"Naw," said Tom. "Didn't scare *me*. Stupid elk's just lucky I didn't have my rifle. Let's go back to the jeep. I'd like some water."

15

Ruthie said nothing, but she couldn't help smiling a little. Tom was not a very good actor.

As they walked back toward the jeep, Ruthie's thoughts returned once more to the old man at Hidden Creek.

"Say, Tom—have you seen a . . . well, a funny-looking stranger around town?" she asked on a sudden impulse.

Tom turned his head sharply. There was a peculiar look in his clear, green eyes—an unexpected coldness that she'd never seen there before. "What do you mean, 'funny-looking'?" he said. A hard edge tinged his voice.

Taken aback by his reaction, Ruthie stammered, "Well . . . well, I don't know. Funny clothes. A . . . a funny way of doing things."

Tom's jaw tightened visibly. "No. I ain't seen anybody like that," he replied curtly.

Ruthie was perplexed. Tom was sometimes blustery and rude, but usually he didn't mean anything by it. She knew his home life was difficult, and that he'd had a strange upbringing. People in Sand Fork referred to Tom's father as "the town drunk," and it was general knowledge that his mother had run off with a drifter when Tom was just a baby. He'd had his troubles; Ruthie knew he'd been caught stealing several times, and he was always in fistfights with the other boys. It did not surprise her that his manners were bad, but this time he seemed truly angry. Could she have said something wrong?

"This stranger. Just what would he look like?" asked Tom, his eyes fixed stonily on some point in the distance.

"I don't know," said Ruthie hesitantly. "Old—with

white hair, and skin like an Indian's. Dressed in a robe, sort of like an Arab."

She began to wonder whether he really *had* seen the stranger in spite of his denial. But why should he lie about it?

"Where did you see him?" Tom demanded.

Ruthie began to feel angry. She didn't like being treated this way. "Why should I tell you?" she jabbed.

His response was explosive and frightening. "Don't play games with me. Tell me where you saw him!"

"I . . . I . . . out at Hidden Creek . . . in the miner's shack . . . just this morning."

"Well, if I were you, Ruthie, I wouldn't go back there, you understand?" His voice was almost a growl. "And another thing." He turned to face her. Beads of perspiration stood out on his forehead, and for an awful moment she thought he was going to grab her. "If you tell anybody else about him, you'll be sorry." With that, he stalked off toward the jeep, leaving her in complete bewilderment.

That night, as she lay in bed looking through her window at the slender crescent of the waning moon, she thought again and again of the stranger and of Tom's puzzling reaction to him. She didn't know what to make of it. Maybe Tom had discovered the old man just as she had, and was trying to protect her from him. But Tom's warning hadn't sounded protective—it had sounded threatening.

She considered the stranger. Though he had frightened her, he had also fascinated her. She remembered what he'd said. "I hear you. Please let me see you." Even though the words were distorted, it wasn't an evil voice. In a way, it was a wonderful voice. It was as smooth as chalk and as clear as mountain water. She couldn't understand Tom. She only knew that there was something very funny going on. As she fell asleep, she made up her mind to go back to Hidden Creek the next day.

In the morning, she brushed Sundust carefully and, after a long struggle, managed to tie a gunnysack full of compost behind his saddle. If that bare patch were really a garden, she was sure the old man could use some fertilizer. It was a good way to show that she'd come in friendship. But at the last minute, remembering the fear that had gripped her and uneasy about Tom's warning, she ran back to the house for her rifle. She was glad when Farmer, the ranch dog, trotted along beside her as she rode through the gate on her way to Hidden Creek Canyon. Farmer was good company, and good protection, too.

It was already ten o'clock when Ruthie, gathering all her courage, approached the miner's shack. She promised herself there would be no hiding this time. She swallowed hard.

As they got nearer, Farmer began to whine, his ears stiff and straight. "What's the matter, boy?" she asked, but a second later, she knew.

Shouts and the sounds of a scuffle came from outside the shack. Without allowing herself time to think about it, Ruthie jumped down from the saddle and pulled her rifle from its case. Her heart pounded as she rushed into the clearing.

There, tumbling about in the dust, locked in combat, were Tom Castor and the stranger. Tom had a knife, and the expression on his face could not be mistaken. Unbelievable as it seemed, he was trying to kill the old man!

TWO

* * * *

Rowen

"**S**TOP it, Tom!" shouted Ruthie.

But Tom and the stranger continued to grapple, rolling over and over on the bare earth.

"Stop it!" she cried once more, though by now she sensed it was futile.

Farmer crouched at the edge of the fray, barking and whining, apparently too confused to choose sides. Ruthie knew just how he felt.

She watched in dismay as Tom pinned the stranger down and lunged at him with a long, shiny hunting knife. With unexpected agility and strength, the old man grabbed Tom's arm and stopped the blade, inches away from his throat. Finally, knowing only that she had to do *something,* Ruthie propped her rifle against a tree and leaped at Tom's back, clenching him around the waist in an effort to pull him away. Dust flew everywhere, choking and blinding her, but still she hung on.

"Leave him alone!" she shouted.

"Get away!" Tom yelled, shoving her forcefully with his elbow.

Ruthie flew backward in a powdery spray of dirt, too agitated to feel any pain.

There was one more thing she could try, though she knew it was a desperate and reckless tactic. Scrambling to her feet, she reached for her rifle. She drew back the bolt, took a cartridge from her shirt pocket, and placed it in the chamber.

"I'm warning you, Tom Castor, stop it!" she cried. Her head was spinning. She didn't like using the rifle this way. It broke every rule her father had so carefully taught her. She did it only because she could see no other way to prevent bloodshed.

She lifted its dully shining barrel until it was aimed at the sky, then pulled the trigger. The crack of the shot was clear and deafening in the morning air.

Tom jumped back and whirled in her direction, the knife still in his hand. But Ruthie had already pulled back the bolt and slipped another cartridge into the chamber.

"All right, Tom. I don't care what this is about, and I won't tell anybody if you don't want me to. But I think you should go home now," she said rapidly, her voice high and quavering. She shoved the bolt forward. It clicked menacingly.

Tom stared at her almost unseeingly, his nostrils flaring, his ruffled hair sticking out in thick red spikes. For a moment, she thought he was going to come after her, but Farmer snarled a warning, baring his long white fangs. Tom hung back.

She pressed the advantage. "Better do what I said! Get away from here!"

Wordlessly, Tom bent to pick up his hat. He walked stiffly toward a motorcycle parked in the shade of a nearby cottonwood, and started it with a fierce kick.

Then, spraying dust in a wide circle, he raced away down the trail. As he disappeared, she heard him give a high, inarticulate cry—whether of rage or anguish she could not tell.

The stranger sat propped on his elbows, coughing and gasping in the dusty air. Ruthie put down her rifle, and without a second's hesitation slapped him firmly between the shoulder blades several times, afraid that he was choking.

"Are you okay?" she asked.

The old man looked up at her, blinking. At once, involuntarily, she took a quick step backward. What was it about his face? There was something wrong about it—something subtly frightening. She stared at him. His eyes were deep blue, almost indigo. She had never seen eyes that color before. But there must have been something else. What?

Farmer approached cautiously, sniffing, his head low. Ruthie patted him uneasily, whispering, "Be good, now, boy. Be good."

The old man lifted a hand and touched one of his ears softly, as if to make sure it was still there. He seemed so dazed that Ruthie began to wonder if Tom had hurt him after all.

"Are you okay?" she repeated.

In reply she received a short burst of the same whistle that had terrified her the day before. With a frightened croak, Ruthie dropped back another two steps and began to consider sprinting toward Sundust again.

But suddenly the whistle turned into words. "What does 'okay' mean?" asked the stranger in an eerie, distorted voice. His accent was thick and unidentifiable.

Ruthie gulped and cleared her throat. "Uh . . . all right. Unharmed. Are you all right?" she faltered.

The stranger's reply came in a language so universal that she understood it at once. He smiled, and Ruthie was immediately spellbound. It was the most incredible smile she had ever seen, transforming his outlandish face as the rising sun transforms the hills of the desert.

"I am okay," he said. "You made a loud noise. In the beginning, I could not hear."

"Oh . . . well, I'm sorry. That was my rifle. Sorry it was so loud." She felt tongue-tied and self-conscious for not having thought of something better to say. But, slowly, the fear was melting away. In its place was a growing fascination.

"I hoped you would return," said the stranger. "You chose a good time." The more he spoke, the more magical his voice seemed—now as smooth as moondust, almost like a song.

"Then you knew I'd been here before?" asked Ruthie, kneeling beside him and taking his arm carefully.

He leaned heavily on her as she helped him to his feet. "Yes. I remembered your sounds," he replied.

His answer was so odd that for a moment Ruthie stood motionless, entirely baffled by it. She had never heard of a person who could recognize someone else's sounds.

Shaking herself, she tried to dismiss the stranger's puzzling remark. "Uh . . . I hope Tom didn't hurt you."

"No, I am not harmed." Vigorously, he brushed the dust from his robe.

"All the same, why don't you sit down for a minute?" Taking his elbow, she guided him toward the rickety porch of the shack.

"If you desire," he said, smiling again. "But I am confused. You helped me. Why?"

"Huh?" said Ruthie incredulously. "Are you joking? Tom would have killed you."

"True. But . . . you know Tom. You do not know me. You helped me. You did not help Tom."

"Look, I don't know how they do things where you come from, but in this country, killing somebody is about the worst thing a person can do. I couldn't just stand there—I *had* to stop him." She looked away toward the dry, rugged outline of the nearby Calico Hills. "Only I can't figure out why he'd want to do it. I mean, Tom Castor's not *that* bad. What could you possibly have done to make him want to kill you?"

The old man turned his hands palms upward and gazed into the sky. "I do not know Tom. I do not know this answer."

Confounded once again by his sheer peculiarity, Ruthie searched his face for signs of a lie. But his features were as impenetrable as stone to her. There was no way of guessing the truth or falsehood of his words. She could only trust the inner voice that said he couldn't smile the way he had if he were a liar.

Just then she felt Sundust, who had walked up behind them, nuzzling her back. She suddenly remembered the bag of compost.

"Oh, I almost forgot," she said, untying the ropes that held the gunnysack to the saddle. She grabbed a corner and tugged the bag to the ground. "I saw your garden the other day and thought maybe you could use this."

"I am a stranger to you, but you bring a gift. You make me feel . . ." He hesitated, obviously searching for a word. "I feel . . . great wonder."

"Gosh," said Ruthie, suddenly warm with embarrassment. "It's just a bag of compost. It's no big deal."

The old man gathered up the hem of his bright robe and knelt to examine the sack. "For my garden?" His laugh was almost a warble. "My garden is bad. I am not a good farmer."

There was a short, sharp bark and the rustle of a wagging tail behind them.

Ruthie laughed. "No, Farmer! We're not talking about you."

"Farmer? That is a strange name for this creature. Does he farm, also?"

Ruthie giggled aloud at this extraordinary remark. "Of course not. He's just a dog. I don't know why we call him Farmer. I guess it *is* a funny name, huh?"

She reached down to help the old man with the bag. "Do you have a name?" she asked.

He lifted the other end. "Yes. I have a name. Do you also?"

"Yes, of course." This was the most bizarre conversation Ruthie had ever had. "But that's not fair. I asked you first," she said as they started toward the garden. "Come on. What's your name?"

"My name is Rowen."

"Rowen," she said softly. She couldn't make it sound quite right. When *he* spoke the name, it was like the whisper of wind in the trees. "That's a beautiful name," she breathed.

"Thank you. What is yours?"

"Oh, just Ruthie. Ruthie Keag. I live on the Bitterbrush Ranch, over in the direction of Sand Fork. Me and my mom and dad. It's only the three of us now, since my brothers left home."

They had reached the garden. "Have you planted anything yet?" she asked.

"I planted some seeds that were on my ship. I have not planted a great number."

"Oh, so you came over on a ship, huh?" She took out her pocketknife and slit one end of the gunnysack. Rich, dark compost spilled out onto the ground. "Where are you from, anyway?"

Rowen's indigo gaze seemed deeper than ever as he replied, "Very far away."

The next day, Ruthie went into town with her parents. Her mother headed for the grocery store, and her father disappeared into the Sand Fork Mercantile in search of a new shovel. But Ruthie had plans of her own, and made straight for Washoe's Feed and Seed.

On the way, she almost tripped over her best friend Kate McGee, who was sitting on the edge of a sunny curb, engrossed in a thick, paperback mystery novel.

"Oh, Ruthie! It's you," said Kate, smiling up at her. "I didn't even see you coming. Boy, is this ever a good book."

"Reading again!" exclaimed Ruthie with a laugh. "Isn't the librarian tired of seeing you yet?"

"Oh, come on," said Kate, her blue eyes sparkling. "I don't read *that* much." She closed the book and tucked it under her arm. "Where are you going?"

"Over to Washoe's. Want to come?"

Kate shrugged. "Sure. What's at Washoe's that's worth coming all the way from the Bitterbrush?"

"Oh, I just came into town with my folks. Thought I'd pick up a few packages of seeds while I'm here."

"Huh!" laughed Kate. "I'd have thought you'd be saving all your money for transistors and that other radio junk."

Ruthie chuckled. Whenever she teased Kate about her books, Kate responded with jabs about electronics.

They opened the door and went up to the counter, where she explained what she wanted to Steve Washoe, the tall Indian man who owned the store.

"It's pretty late in the year to start a garden," said Steve as he handed Ruthie the packets of seeds. He was smiling.

"I know," she replied. "But not *too* late. If I stay away from carrots and corn, I think I can still get something before September."

He smiled widely, his dark eyes twinkling as he said, "You learn fast. We'll make a good farmer out of you yet. Maybe you should buy a pair of overalls and a straw hat, too."

Kate giggled and nudged Ruthie with her elbow. Ruthie grinned, her cheeks reddening. She liked Steve, even though he often teased her.

"Well, we gotta be going," she said, rolling up the top of the paper bag he had given her. "Mom and Dad are probably waiting. Thanks a lot, Mr. Washoe."

"My pleasure," he called after them as they hurried out the door.

On the main street of Sand Fork the sun beat down like a hammer, and a hot, dry wind had come up from the west. Ruthie and Kate walked toward the jeep, parked at the curb a few steps away.

"Boy, do I ever have a story to tell you," said Ruthie. The wind had blown some of the hair loose from her long, dark braids, and she groped for the door handle through a fog of chocolaty curls. "Let's sit in the jeep for a minute."

"Okay," agreed Kate.

But just as Ruthie swung the door open, something

26

hit her shoulder from behind so hard that she lost her balance and dropped the bag of seeds on the sidewalk. She heard Kate gasp in surprise.

Before she could gather her wits, the bag was rolling helter-skelter down the street. As she chased it, angry and embarrassed, she heard a loud voice behind her.

"Hey! Ruthie Keag! Why can't you mind your own business?" The wind carried the words like hot bullets. People passing by stopped to see what the ruckus was about.

Ruthie snatched up the bag and whirled furiously to face her tormentor. There stood Tom Castor, his eyes glittering with ferocity.

She felt the blood drain out of her face as she remembered the mindless, animal cry he'd let forth while racing away from the miner's shack. What if he had the knife with him this time? No rifle could help her now.

THREE

* * * *

The Night Excursion

TOM CASTOR walked up and gave Ruthie another little shove backward. "Why can't you keep out of things that don't concern you, Ruthie?" The corners of his mouth twisted downward in an ugly scowl.

Anger and indignation made Ruthie forget her fear. "You've got a lot of nerve, Tom," she cried. "What was I supposed to do? Stand there and let you kill him?"

Before Ruthie knew what had happened, she was lying on her back in the road, her mouth filled with the rusty taste of her own blood. She touched her lower lip. Her fingers came away red and sticky.

Infuriated, she leaped to her feet and rushed at him, striking out with her fists in a blind effort to repay him. But he stopped her easily. A single push from his lanky arm sent her sprawling in the dirt again.

She heard Kate yelling. "Somebody stop it. Help!" Ruthie fought to keep back tears as the paper bag tore open and packets of seeds spilled out into the wind.

Suddenly, Steve Washoe was towering above them, one hand on Tom's shoulder and the other balled into a fist. He lowered his head ominously. "What do you think you're doing?" he thundered. The look on Tom's face changed from anger to fear. "Get out of here!" Tom turned and fled down the street without another word.

Ruthie sat down shakily on the curb. Her body fizzed with adrenaline. Her heart thudded, and she could not keep her hands from trembling as she felt her swollen lip.

Quietly, Steve bent down and picked up the scattered seed packets, then offered her a freshly ironed handkerchief.

"I'll go get some ice," Kate volunteered, and dashed down the street toward the Sand Fork Café.

"What was *that* all about?" asked Steve.

"Oh," said Ruthie, wincing as she moved her tender jaw, "he's mad at me because I caught him fighting with somebody and tried to break it up." The explanation was carefully worded. She was now certain that she didn't want the story of Rowen spread about town.

Steve shook his head, his straight black hair sparkling in the sun. "That boy's gonna come to no good."

Just then, Ruthie's father strode up with two new shovels slung across his shoulders. "What's goin' on here?" he asked, frowning.

"That crazy Tom Castor," said Steve. "You wait and see, he's gonna be worse than his father!" Glowering like a thunderhead, Steve shook his fist.

Mr. Keag turned to Ruthie. "What happened?"

"Nothin'," said Ruthie, still trying to control her shaking hands. "I'm okay."

Kate returned breathlessly with a bowl of ice cubes.

Rosie, the café owner, Mr. Sheldon, the pharmacist, and Ruthie's mother were not far behind.

"Here, Ruthie," said Kate, wrapping an ice cube in the handkerchief. "This'll help the swelling."

"Thanks," said Ruthie, gratefully accepting the homemade compress.

Mr. Keag chuckled dryly. "Nothin' happened, huh?" He put his shovels down and gently lifted Ruthie's chin, then looked at Steve Washoe questioningly.

"That boy's loco," said Steve. "He walked up and started shouting and punching—nothin' I could see to start it."

"Ruthie!" cried Mrs. Keag, rushing up to them. She set her two bags of groceries on the sidewalk and bent to examine Ruthie's lip.

"Is that true, Ruthie? Tom started it?" asked Mr. Keag.

"Oh, I don't know, Dad," said Ruthie miserably. The ice had made her lip sting, and she was uncomfortably aware of the small crowd that had gathered around her. "He's mad because I stopped him from beating up an old man yesterday."

"What old man?" said her father, raising his eyebrows.

Ruthie was suddenly afraid that she had made a serious slip. She felt somehow protective about Rowen. It occurred to her that he was a squatter on the land at Hidden Creek and that he had no legal right to be there. She was certain that if word got around, the sheriff would run him out of the shack.

"Oh, just some poor old prospector . . . a stranger. I don't even know who he was." Ruthie looked down at her feet nervously.

"That boy!" said Mrs. Keag, shaking her head.

31

"He's as wild as a tumbleweed. His father should have taken the time to give him a good swat now and then long before this."

Ruthie's father shook his head. "John Castor's more interested in whiskey than he is in his son. It's no wonder Tom's in trouble all the time." He picked up the new shovels again. "Come on. Let's get on home. And Steve—thanks a lot."

Ruthie was about to try her unsteady legs when Kate piped up, "Say, would it be all right if Ruthie spent the night at my house? We could ride my horse out to the Bitterbrush tomorrow morning when it's time for her to go home."

Ruthie smiled, delighted at the idea. "That would be great. Can I, Mom? Dad?"

Ruthie's mother looked at her worriedly. "Are you sure you're okay?"

"And is it all right with Kate's folks?" added Mr. Keag.

"I'll call my mom right now," said Kate, and dashed away to find a telephone.

"I'm fine, Mom. He didn't really hurt me," said Ruthie.

In a moment, Kate was back with good news. Everything was fine; Ruthie could stay as long as she liked.

When the crowd was gone and Ruthie's parents had driven away in the jeep, Kate turned to her and said in a low voice, "Ruthie, I'm so glad you're staying over. I'm worried. There's something very funny going on around here, and Tom Castor's right in the middle of it."

"What do you mean?" asked Ruthie, wondering whether Kate, too, had noticed Tom's unusual behavior in the past several days. "I mean, I agree—there's something funny happening. But you must have more to go on than just Tom's punching me."

"I'll say," Kate breathed, shaking her head. "Tom punching a girl right in broad daylight in the middle of Main Street is crazy enough . . . but there are other things."

"Like what?" asked Ruthie.

"Well, the biggest thing is this. Did you know that the general store was broken into last week?"

"Yeah, I heard something about it."

"There were only a few things taken—none of them very valuable. A pair of earplugs was missing, and some men's work clothes. Everybody thinks some tramp must have done it."

Kate glanced around furtively, then went on in a whisper. "Ruthie, Tom Castor did it. I saw him."

Ruthie stopped in the middle of the sidewalk, suddenly stiffening as she recalled Rowen's sensitive ears; Rowen and his shining robes that would mark him as a stranger on any street in America.

"What do you suppose Tom would want with earplugs and work clothes?" Ruthie said slowly, afraid to admit that the real answer might be something very unpleasant indeed.

"You probably wouldn't believe me if I told you," Kate muttered. "I can hardly believe it myself."

Ruthie waited for Kate to go on, but her friend did not continue. "Well?" said Ruthie, fighting to keep her voice down. "Tell me."

"I can't. I'll never be able to explain. If you'll trust me, I'll take you someplace where you can see for yourself. But we have to wait until dark."

* * *

In the evening stillness, as the last hint of daylight faded from a vivid, cloudless sky, Kate and Ruthie set out on a walk through Sand Fork.

As silently as two mice they stepped along Main Street, past darkened storefronts and lonely neon signs that buzzed like angry flies. They passed the theater, where the scent of warm popcorn drifted out to the sidewalk. Then Kate led them abruptly down a dark side street in which the only signs of life were a distant glow in the window of a bar and the deep bass notes of a jukebox playing country music.

"Where are we going?" whispered Ruthie. "This alley gives me the creeps."

"You'll see. Come on."

Before they reached the bar, Kate changed direction again, this time leading the way down a grimy service road lined on one side with run-down shacks. She stopped in the bushes behind one of them.

"Do you know where we are?" Kate asked.

"Yeah. We're behind Commercial Row, in the roughest part of town," Ruthie answered. "And the sooner we get out of here the better!"

"Not yet," Kate whispered vehemently. "First you have to see." She pulled Ruthie deeper into the shadows. "This is Tom Castor's house. I followed him here the other night after I saw him rob the store."

Ruthie stared at the grim little tar-paper shack. A rusty, tin chimney protruded from the patched roof like a crooked finger. The weathered, ill-fitting door hung precariously on cracked leather hinges. She had always known that the Castors lived in poverty, but she had never actually seen how bad it was before. She was appalled.

Without a sound, Kate crept out of the darkness toward a dirty little window where pale yellow light seeped out from the slats of a dilapidated blind. Slowly, she raised her head until a band of shadow made a raccoon's mask across her eyes. She turned to Ruthie with a finger on her lips and beckoned. Her face was pale, and in the eerie lamplight Ruthie saw goose bumps on Kate's bare arms. What had she seen?

Ruthie tried to swallow the cottony feeling in her mouth as she crawled out of the bushes to crouch beside Kate at the window. At first it was hard to see anything through the narrow slits of the blind. But, in a moment, she realized that she was looking into a kind of living room. There were two people in the room. One of them was Tom, slumped sullenly in a battered chair. He played idly with a pocketknife, throwing it into the gray wooden floor with a twang, bending to retrieve it, throwing it again.

But it was the other figure who held her entranced. She felt the coldness of perspiration on her forehead as she looked at the man. Dressed in workman's clothes that were too large for him, he lay dozing on the torn and faded sofa. Ruthie stared. He was short and slender, thinner than even the lanky Tom. Though he looked too young for it, he was nearly bald. Fine, bone-colored hair grew in a shaggy band above his small, round ears. He's got a sunburn, Ruthie thought as she looked at his face and hands. But she knew it wasn't true. She recognized that dull red coloring. And in a cold, inexplicable way she was certain that if he opened his eyes they would be dark, dark blue, like a deep lake on a moonless night. He could have been Rowen's brother.

Kate leaned closer to Ruthie and said in a barely au-

dible whisper, "I've never seen anybody like that before. I don't know who he is."

Ruthie grimaced, motioning frantically for Kate to be quiet. But it was too late. The stranger's hearing was just as acute as Rowen's. His eyes blinked open and he sat up swiftly. Through the glass, Ruthie could just hear him say in the peculiar accent she had known he would have, "What was that? Someone is outside the window."

"Huh?" cried Tom, leaping to his feet.

"Run!" whispered Ruthie urgently, and gave Kate a little push. Wildly, they scrambled to their feet and pounded down the alleyway as fast as their legs could carry them.

They had just turned the corner when the door of the shack slammed. Tom's voice floated thinly across the clear, night air. "Who's there?"

"Faster!" cried Ruthie. She was certain she heard the slap-slap-slap of boots on the pavement behind them.

FOUR

* * * *

Danger in
Sand Fork

Rᴜᴛʜɪᴇ and Kate rushed wildly down the dark street.
By the time they had passed the neon sign of the
bar, Ruthie's legs felt as if they were on fire. Beside
her, Kate gasped for breath and cried weakly, "I can't
keep up! I can't!"

"Come on! Come on!" Ruthie croaked, grabbing
Kate's arm and pulling. The strong, rapid slap of boots
on pavement was undeniable now. Turning her head
briefly, Ruthie caught a glimpse of Tom Castor not half
a block behind them, his face shining with sweat under
the streetlamp. They were losing the race!

As they rounded the corner and headed down Main
Street, something clicked in Ruthie's frantic mind. In
front of the theater, she stopped so suddenly that Kate
skidded to keep from hitting her.

"Ruthie! What are you doing? Let's get out of here!"
Kate shouted, her voice rough with the effort of breathing.

"Trust me!" Ruthie whispered as she tore a worn

39

five-dollar bill from her pocket. "Two, please! Hurry!" she said to the woman in the ticket booth, her voice high and uneven as she strained to keep from shouting.

"Ruthie! He's coming!" Kate cried.

For an instant, Ruthie thought the clerk had not heard. Only the skillful flicking of the nail file in the woman's fingers revealed that she was even awake. "The movie's already started, you know," she finally drawled, without looking up.

"I don't care! Just give me two tickets! Please!" Ruthie pleaded.

For the first time the woman looked at Ruthie. "You won't get your money's worth, and we don't give refunds," she said, resting her chin on the back of her hand.

"We don't care. We just want to see the end of the movie." Ruthie could hardly stand still.

"All right," said the clerk, shaking her head. Two tickets snapped out of a slot in the counter.

"Thanks!" cried Ruthie, snatching the tickets. "Come on!" She pulled Kate through the glass doors into the lobby.

"Hey! What about your change?" called the clerk.

"Keep it!" Ruthie felt a new jolt of fear as she spied Tom dashing around the corner onto Main. Without ceremony, she thrust Kate before her through the curtain and into the dark theater.

Ruthie hesitated a moment as her eyes adjusted to the ghostly light of the screen. She almost cried out in dismay as she looked around. The theater was nearly empty. There was no chance of hiding in the audience as she had planned.

"Now what?" Kate whispered raggedly.

40

"Just let me think a second," Ruthie muttered, pressing a hand to her damp forehead.

She felt as if she were in the midst of a bad dream. For a long, terrible moment, her mind was a blank. She stared down the aisle toward the front of the theater. The doors on either side of the movie screen had glowing, green signs above them that said "EXIT." She knew they led into narrow alleyways where the only chance of escape would be to run out to Main Street again. That would leave them right back where they had started. But there was a third door, closer to the screen than the other two. She had seen it before, and she knew it was labeled with a small sign, "EMPLOYEES ONLY."

"This way," she whispered to Kate, and hurried down the aisle toward the third door.

Her hands were slick with sweat as she found the knob and turned it frantically. Before she had time for second thoughts, she pushed the door open and slipped through it, closing it silently after Kate.

They stood noiselessly, taking in the unfamiliar surroundings behind the door. They were in a small, square chamber at the foot of a short flight of stairs. A single, dim light bulb lit the stairway just enough so they could make out a large, dark entryway at the top.

Holding a finger to her lips, Ruthie motioned Kate to follow her, and started up the stairs. At the top, she realized with sudden hope that the entryway led into a dark, open space behind the screen. She peeked around the corner.

This close, the screen was gigantic. The image of the movie shown through it, and the actors moved about like colossal monsters in a changing sea of bright and dark colors. Three speakers twice as tall as Ruthie

41

loomed like ghostly beasts in the shadows. The noise was deafening.

Nonetheless, Ruthie was certain that the forbidding space behind the screen offered them the safest hiding place in the theater. As they stood in the wings, Kate shrank back into the shadows. Though Ruthie motioned her forward, she seemed too frightened to move. At last, Ruthie grabbed her arm and tugged her out into the turmoil of sound and light.

As they crept toward the center of the screen, Ruthie dropped to all fours in alarm. The screen had thousands of tiny, perfectly arranged holes in it. To her amazement, she could dimly see the audience and the entire theater through those holes. She held her breath. If *she* could see *them,* perhaps *they* could see *her.* She studied the scattered faces, but there were no frowns of suspicion, no fingers pointing up at her. Everyone on the other side seemed engrossed in the movie. If anyone could see her, there were no signs of it. She sighed with relief, slumping against the big center speaker. She could feel it vibrating on her back. Kate crawled slowly up beside her. Ruthie noticed small beads of sweat on Kate's cheeks. Her hair was stringy with moisture from their nightmarish dash through the streets.

Ruthie stared at the unfinished concrete walls, streaked with water stains from many seasons of desert thundershowers. Dismantled theater chairs were stacked like firewood against the furthest wall, and everything was covered with a soft, thick layer of dust. There was a chilling, abandoned look about the place; it was clear that the theater staff went behind the screen only when it was absolutely necessary. Shivering, she understood why.

Kate suddenly tugged at her sleeve. When Ruthie looked over at her, she made small, frantic motions toward the audience. As Ruthie peered out at the theater, her heart once again began to bang crazily. There was Tom Castor, prowling among the seats! He was looking for them. They hadn't escaped yet.

She dared not move as she watched him striding along the aisles, stopping to glare angrily down the few rows where seats were occupied. His face was terrifying in the lurid glare of the projector. Against her will, she thought of the huge, wolflike wild dog that had preyed on their chickens the year before. She had felt just the same when she wandered sleepily out onto the porch, only to be jerked awake by the sight of the massive dog standing like a gray phantom against the clear stars of the desert. But this time, Ruthie's father was not here to save her, and she shuddered at the thought of what might happen if Tom found her.

Fate must have been on her side. For, just then, an usher strode down the aisle with a dim flashlight, and after a few seconds of what must have been a whispered argument, he hustled Tom out of the theater roughly. For the first time in what seemed like hours, Ruthie relaxed. She and Kate exchanged exhausted smiles of relief. But deep inside, Ruthie was afraid that the chase was not over. Tom Castor was apparently out to get her, and she feared that he wouldn't stop trying.

In the morning, Ruthie helped Kate saddle her horse, Pearl, for the ride back to the Bitterbrush Ranch.

"Tom acts like he really hates you, Ruthie," said Kate, as she rummaged through a box of tack.

"I know," Ruthie replied, shaking her head. "I wish he'd just leave me alone." She touched her lip gingerly.

43

The swelling from yesterday's confrontation had gone down during the night, leaving a tender, bluish bruise as a reminder.

"You never did tell me just what happened with that old prospector—you know, the one Tom was fighting with when you stopped him." Kate brushed Pearl's flank with long, smooth strokes as she spoke.

"Yeah, I know," said Ruthie. "We were interrupted." She sat down on a bale of new straw, wondering if she should tell Kate the real story. All night she had tossed and turned, unable to stop thinking about Rowen and the stranger at Tom's house. She was certain the two were connected, but she didn't know exactly how. One part of her wanted desperately to share the mystery with Kate, for it seemed only fair to tell everything after their narrow escape in the theater. Still, she hesitated, for she had an uncomfortable feeling that the more anyone knew about the situation, the greater their peril. Ruthie didn't want to get her friend into any more trouble if she could avoid it.

Ruthie helped Kate lift the saddle onto Pearl's back. "Well, there's not much to tell," she said. "I rode out to the prospector's shack at Hidden Creek the other day, just for fun. And when I got there, I found Tom in a fistfight with an old man—a stranger. Probably just a desert drifter." She trailed off, hoping Kate would let her leave it at that.

Kate cinched the saddle briskly. "Well, I wish I could figure out how that funny-looking guy at Castors' is connected with all this craziness of Tom's. I'm positive he's got something to do with it."

"Yeah," Ruthie replied distantly. "I feel the same way." That much, at least, was the whole truth.

Kate mounted the horse and offered Ruthie a hand

44

up. They spoke very little as they jounced along the dusty road to the Bitterbrush. Kate's lips were pressed together in a thin line and her eyes were fastened on some invisible point in the far-off hills. Ruthie knew Kate was puzzling over the few facts she had managed to gather about Tom and the stranger. Ruthie felt guilty that she hadn't told Kate everything she knew. But she was determined to keep her part of the information secret awhile longer.

Though Ruthie invited her to stay for the afternoon, Kate turned the offer down. As they stood on the front porch after lunch Kate explained, "I'd sure like to stay, but I just can't. Mom will want me home in plenty of time to help with supper, and it's a long ride."

As they walked Pearl out to the gate and Kate swung up into the saddle, she looked down and said, "If you think of anything, you know . . . anything that might help explain about Tom, call me. And I'll call you if I think of anything. Okay?"

"Sure," answered Ruthie, turning away to stroke Pearl's nose.

"Ruthie." She felt Kate's hand on her shoulder. "Promise?"

"Promise," Ruthie replied, averting her eyes.

With a flick of the reins, Kate was off, galloping back down the road to town, twisting in the saddle to wave good-bye.

No sooner had Kate disappeared than Ruthie was sprinting back toward the barn with only one idea in mind. Hidden Creek and the mystery of Rowen beckoned to her like a deep and wonderful cavern. Even though it frightened her a little, she burned with curiosity. She would ride out to the miner's shack without a minute's delay. She would find the old man and get him to tell her the real story, once and for all.

But just as she sped past the house on her way to the corral, she heard her mother calling from the porch. "Ruthie, where are you going?"

"I'm gonna take Sundust out for a ride," she shouted in reply.

Mrs. Keag put her hands on her hips. "Well, that can wait. I need you to help me in the kitchen for a while."

"Aw, Mom!" Ruthie cried anxiously. "Do I *have* to?"

"Ruthie Keag, behave yourself! Yes, you have to, and you should be glad to do it."

Ruthie held back her disappointment as well as she could. Still, her face felt hot and flushed, and it was all she could do to reply weakly, "Okay, Mom."

She spent the next hour halfheartedly peeling and chopping zucchini squash for relish and pickles. It seemed as if there were an unending supply of the slender, green vegetables arranged beside her in a bottomless basket.

"Ruthie, you've got to cut these into smaller pieces," her mother chided when she tried to speed up the process by increasing the size of the chunks.

"Yes, Mom," she replied meekly.

But before long, the pieces were too large again, and after three scoldings, Mrs. Keag gave a sigh of resignation. "All right. Go on. Get out of here and go take your ride. Goodness knows, you're no help to me in this mood."

"Oh, thanks, Mom!" Ruthie cried, jumping up from the cutting board and throwing the knife down with a clatter.

"Don't be late for dinner," her mother called as Ruthie scrambled up the stairs to her bedroom.

"I won't," she answered, secretly crossing her fingers. It would be close. The ride to Hidden Creek and back usually took three hours at an easy trot. But she knew Sundust could do better than that if he had to.

She picked up the packages of vegetable seeds, grabbed her saddlebags from the bedpost, and ran for the barn. Sundust was delighted at the idea of an outing, and stood patiently at the corral fence while she put on his bridle and threw a blanket over his creamy tan back. She tossed the saddlebags across the lower part of his neck, then used the fence for a ladder as she mounted him. She rode nearly as well bareback as she did with a saddle. On this ride, every minute was precious to her, and the saddle was an unnecessary luxury.

She touched her heels to Sundust's sides as she took the reins, and with a soft whinny he trotted down the road toward the sagebrush plain at the foot of the hills.

There was no sign of Rowen when she reached the shack at Hidden Creek. His strange bucket lay on its side near the garden patch, where the newly turned earth blew in dry wisps on the breeze.

"Rowen," she called. But there was no answer, only the creak of an unfastened window shutter as it swung out and back on its half-rotted canvas hinges. She looked around uneasily. Thoughts of Tom and his hunting knife flooded her mind.

She had gone all the way around Rowen's tiny house when she heard cracking twigs and the swish of leaves as someone came up the bank from the creek. Her heart beat like a kettledrum as she called Rowen one more time.

Ruthie watched apprehensively as a disheveled figure staggered out of the brush toward her. It was Rowen, his ordinarily ruddy face a distressing white, and his lovely robe wet and spattered with mud!

47

FIVE

* * * *

The Magnificent Secret

Rᴜᴛʜɪᴇ jumped down from Sundust's back without stopping to tether him, and rushed toward Rowen.

"What happened?" she cried. His breath came in tearing gasps. His gait was so unsteady that she took him by the arm the instant she reached him. Tom Castor. Tom Castor. The name repeated itself in her mind like a tolling bell. She had no doubt that he was responsible for this.

"Very fast . . . in my dwelling . . . an object I need . . . ," Rowen wheezed.

"Should I get something for you? Is that it?"

"I am not able . . . to tell you . . . what it looks like."

He staggered further in the direction of the shack with a look of desperate concentration. It must have been an effort of tremendous willpower; his face was now a frightening ashen color, and he was clearly on the ragged margin of consciousness.

With a strength she didn't know she possessed,

49

Ruthie threw one of his arms over her shoulders and half dragged him to the shack. She kicked open the flimsy door. With his free arm, Rowen stretched toward a rickety shelf that hung on the wall near the rusty wood stove. Ruthie helped him to reach the shelf, hoping that he could still recognize and use whatever it was that he was looking for so frantically.

He seized a small wooden box, groped through it feverishly, and at last held up a small metallic cylinder. Slipping his hand through the loose folds of his robe, he made a sharp, jabbing motion. Suddenly she felt him go limp in her grasp. As she lowered him to the floor, his hand fell away from the cylinder, revealing the most startling sight she had ever seen. The cylinder, which now began to hiss ominously, was stuck into a metal fitting in the skin of Rowen's chest!

Ruthie drew back with a gasping scream. For an endless moment she crouched as if frozen on the hard dirt floor, waiting for something to happen. Her image of Rowen as the eccentric and harmless foreigner melted like butter left in the sun. In its place was a blind fear of the incomprehensible. Who was this old man? Indeed, *what* was he? And what did Tom Castor know about him that *she* did not?

Rowen's breathing began to slow and the purplish color of his face dissolved in stages—first to a pale cream, and then back to its usual brick red. Whatever was in the cylinder seemed to be helping. Still, he lay unmoving.

She glanced around the shack uneasily. She had been inside it before, but only when its residents were spiders and field mice. Now it was full of unfamiliar objects. Two pictures hung on the wall—not paintings, not drawings, not exactly photographs. One was a plain, black background, flecked with random white dots of many sizes. The other resembled a map or a landscape or a combination of the two—an other-worldly scene of jutting mountains and colorful prairies. There was a kind of long, narrow hammock anchored in one corner. In the middle of the room were two sleek chairs that would have looked more at home in an expensive sports car. There were other items, too, most of them unrecognizable to her. Only one article was familiar, though it looked oddly out of place—a worn copy of *Webster's* dictionary. Ruthie felt as if she were watching a play in which the curtain had accidentally been raised between acts. She was seeing things she was never meant to.

Rowen groaned softly. For a few seconds he stared up at the ceiling, blinking as if dense fog hung before his eyes. Ruthie considered her choices. She could answer her sudden misgivings—get up, walk out the door, ride away with Sundust, and never come back. But that would mean leaving the great mystery unsolved. She would never know who this strange little man was, or what had brought him to this wretched place on the edge of a broad, bleak desert. And there was something yet more important. He had been kind to her.

When Rowen tried to sit up, she helped him. The metal cylinder protruded from his breast like a signpost. Grasping it in his hand, he pulled it out and looked at her with an odd mixture of sadness and defiance.

"I am sorry. I wish you had not seen this. I will not force you to stay any longer here."

"I don't mind," said Ruthie in her gentlest voice. "I think I'll stay awhile anyway, if it's okay with you."

A smile crossed his face swiftly, like the sun peeping out from behind clouds, and he replied, "Yes. It is okay."

Ruthie would have helped him to his feet, but he stood up quickly by himself before she could move.

"Maybe you should take it easy for a minute. Let me get you some water from my canteen."

"Yes," said Rowen, weaving slightly as he stood before her. "I will sit down."

Outside, Sundust stood where Ruthie had left him, unusually obedient. Ruthie patted his neck and led him to a small tree, where she tethered him. She took down the canteen. Then, opening a pocket on the outside of one saddlebag, she took out the seeds, packaged in their colorful paper envelopes. These she slipped into her shirt pocket for safekeeping, remembering how the wind had carried them down the street the day before.

On one of Rowen's shelves, she found a cup with a funny, twisted handle. Filling it with the cool water, she handed it to him silently. She had too many questions. It was hard to decide which ones could be asked and which ones could not.

She pulled the seeds from her pocket and handed them to him inelegantly. "I came out today to bring you these. They're for your garden." She hadn't said any of the things she wanted to. She felt slightly ashamed, and turned away awkwardly.

The paper packets crinkled as Rowen examined them. "You are a remarkable person, Ruthie Keag."

She laughed nervously, still unable to face him.

"I will plant these seeds with great honor. Twice you have saved my life. If seeds could save me now, it would be three times."

"What do you mean—if seeds could save you?" The ominous tone of those words abruptly diminished everything except her concern for him. "Save you from

52

what?" Half a dozen possible answers rattled in her skull like skeleton fingers.

But Rowen's reply took her by surprise. "From the weakness of my body."

He must have understood the look of perplexity on Ruthie's face, for after a moment he added, "This is not a good place for me. I am ill."

In her confusion Ruthie blurted, "Well of course you don't feel good! You're camped out here in the middle of nowhere with a measly sagebrush fire and no decent food, and some creep is trying to kill you. Why don't you move into town?"

It was as if the floodgates of a dam had opened. "Darn it, Rowen! Why won't you let me help you? Any idiot can see you're in a lot of trouble. You won't tell me anything!"

"I do not desire to hurt you. You honor me with your kindness," said Rowen softly. "But I cannot live among your people, Ruthie Keag. Never. I believe that you can see why, if you wish to."

Suddenly, Ruthie was shaking like a young aspen tree in the wind. "Why *can't* you live in town? That other guy does—the one who looks like you."

Rowen half rose from his chair, his face suddenly taut. "Someone who looks like me? You have seen this person yourself?"

"Yeah—yesterday through the window of Tom Castor's house. And he looks enough like you to be your brother. Don't tell me you didn't know that?"

"Tarnum! He survived, then!" whispered Rowen. He dropped back into his seat, suddenly pale again.

Ruthie's heart was going much too fast, and her ears had begun to ring. "Who's Tarnum?" she cried. "You're scaring me!"

53

"I do not wish to frighten you, but . . ." Rowen contemplated her sadly. "Why do you not ask first, 'Who is Rowen?'? For I believe that is more important to you."

"All right, then. Who is Rowen?"

"But you already know, do you not?"

"No! I don't know!" Ruthie shouted stubbornly. "Tell me!"

But Rowen made no reply. He sat before her like an eerie statue, still too pale, his robe glimmering.

"I don't understand. It doesn't make sense. *You* don't make any sense!" Even as the words tumbled out, a thought floated up through her consciousness like a gleaming bubble from the bottom of a pond.

He sat motionless in his chair. A beam of light from the setting sun played against his face. There was something wrong about his ears. She remembered noticing it that first day. They were too small, too round.

Outside, a bullfrog in the willows by the water began his evening song, an unearthly, rhythmic bleating that turned her blood to ice. One more time, she wanted to run away—not from Rowen, but from what he represented. Instead, she sat transfixed.

"You know, do you not?" he repeated softly. "You see now what you did not wish to see."

There it was again, that strange combination of sadness and pride that she'd sensed in him before.

"Look at me," he whispered. "My eyes, my skin. I am not like you. Look at my clothing. Listen to me. My voice is the voice of no human. My tongue is the wrong shape for the languages of humankind. Do you not wonder why I am here, why Tarnum is here?"

She moved forward on the edge of her chair. "You're not a human being, are you? You're something else! You're from *somewhere else!*"

SIX

* * * *

Tarnum

ROWEN looked at her wordlessly. For a long moment, Ruthie was too stunned by her discovery to speak. She was filled with wonder, terror, and strange delight all at the same time.

She looked again at his ears that were the wrong shape, his eyes that were an impossible color. She now realized it was more than the vivid, deep blue that had always bothered her. His pupils, small and barely darker than the irises, were almost *square*. She gazed at his sun-brick skin—not quite the color of any human complexion.

"But you said you came over on a ship—" she began, and swallowed suddenly. He had never said *what kind of ship*. She was the one who'd assumed it was a seagoing vessel from some exotic land on the other side of the ocean. She had never dreamed it might be a starship, traveling the oceans of space!

Something must have gone terribly wrong. Why else would he be camped here at Hidden Creek, sick and trying to scrape a garden out of the desert clay?

She could hardly imagine what had led him here, or what kept him from leaving. She knew only that she wanted to help him in whatever way she could. She wanted it more than anything else.

"Rowen," she began timidly, engulfed by embarrassment and regret for the foolish things she had said to him. "I don't blame you if you want me to go away. I guess I've been acting pretty dumb. But if I can help somehow . . . you know, I'd like that. I'd like it a lot."

Rowen gazed at her awhile longer, the deep worry lines in his face softening to a trace of a smile. "Of one thing I am certain," he said at last. "I do not want you to go away. Stay as long as you wish, please. Come here as often as you like."

"Oh, I will! I promise I will!"

"But you do not yet know how great my trouble is. Perhaps you will be sorry."

"It doesn't matter. I wouldn't care if it were the worst trouble in the world. I'd still help you."

"There is danger, my friend. Danger even to your life, perhaps. The one called Tom has come here twice since you first frightened him away. I heard his noises. I was barely able to hide from him in time. I am in Tarnum's path; if you help me, you will be in his path also. Tarnum is desperate. He will do what he must do. And little time remains."

A chill went up her spine as she remembered the midnight chase through town. Yet Rowen's words changed nothing. She had known for some time that this was no baby's game. Tom Castor and Tarnum were obviously playing for keeps.

"It still doesn't matter," she said. "I'm with you for as long as you want me. But I *would* like to know who Tarnum is, and why he's after you."

"That is a question with many sides," said Rowen. And turning toward the window with a faraway look, he told her the most incredible tale she had ever heard.

They came from the second planet of Theta Scorpi, a yellow star of little note in the constellation Scorpius. Ruthie found the name of the planet almost unpronounceable. The closest she could manage was "Seldor," which was far removed from the chirping trill Rowen used when he said the word.

Rowen spoke of a vast galactic society, of which Seldor was only a small part. He described whole planets famous for their agriculture, or their mining, or their fine cloths or spices. There were hundreds of great and little worlds, each of them noteworthy in one way or another.

Seldor was noted for its scholars and adventurers. Nearly always, it was Seldorians who broke the new ground—discovered and then studied new worlds, mapped continents and oceans, catalogued life forms, and, once in a great while, stumbled across unknown civilizations. Earth was a recent and very important find for Seldor. The number and variety of different cultures on this one small planet astounded all the galaxy.

The Seldorians sent teams of scientist-explorers. There was a group of planetologists to gather information about the new planet's geology, analyze its atmosphere, map its moon and continents and seas. There were biologists whose task it was to study and document all the life forms of the Earth. But the most exciting job of all went to the cognitologists—the scientists whose specialty was the study of intelligent beings. It was to this last team that Rowen belonged.

"I have seen the double suns rise in the crystal

cities of Aldebaran Four," he said in a voice at once hushed and excited. "I have lived in the golden caves of the bushmen of Mirfak; learned the fragrant languages of Gamma Hydri." With a sad little laugh, he added, "I have studied the tower dwellings of humans, on the ocean shores of Earth. Perhaps that does not matter much now."

Ruthie tried to imagine herself in Rowen's position. What would it be like to live in a crude camp unimaginably distant from the planet of her birth, where the sun and the sky were unfamiliar colors, and the cities were meaningless sculptures on the bright horizon? What would it be like if home were nothing more than a dot of light occasionally visible in the cold night sky? What if she knew she might never get back?

"Rowen, something went wrong, didn't it? An accident or something. You're stranded here, aren't you?" she whispered.

"Perhaps it was an accident. Perhaps it was not," he said.

Ruthie gazed at him anxiously. Was it anger or remorse that etched his deeply lined face? "This accident . . . did Tarnum have something to do with it?"

"I think, in some way, all of us are to blame. There were only four of us. Tarnum and Porix and I, and Jid, poor Jid. We should, perhaps, have been more kind about Tarnum. Perhaps we should have forgiven him. He is young. He desires fame. What he did we could have put right again. Perhaps we were too hard."

"What did he do?" Ruthie asked.

"He stole a small object of great importance—a thing that belonged to the people of Earth. The oath of the scholar forbids it. We thought only of the oath. In our hardness, we did not think of Tarnum. So if Tarnum killed, all of us were the seed of it."

"You mean he *killed* someone?" Ruthie exclaimed.

"Yes. First Porix, then Jid. Rowen also, if his plan had gone well."

"My gosh! He must be crazy!"

"He is desperate. That which he might lose means more to him than the lives of others."

"But I don't understand. Stealing, that's one thing. But murder's something else. Hasn't he just gotten himself into worse trouble?"

"Perhaps. And perhaps not. The rules of our home are like the rules of yours concerning such matters. To kill someone is a great wrong. Yet if the courts of Seldor never discover the crimes of Tarnum, to him it will be as if none of it had happened."

Slowly, pieces of the story fell into place. Ruthie began to see glimpses of the whole, sordid affair. Tarnum was an ambitious young scientist on his way to the top of the ladder. He was taking part in an important expedition to a newly discovered world. There were artifacts everyplace, any one of them worth a fortune in the right circles. So he'd knuckled under. He'd taken something. What could it have been? Whatever it was, he had probably planned to sell it when he returned to Seldor, for a lot of cash, or perhaps in exchange for favors from some person with influence. That alone disgusted Ruthie, and she understood how angry the other members of the team must have been when the secret was accidentally discovered.

But Tarnum didn't stop there. His career would probably have been finished when his superiors found out about the theft. So he decided to make sure that would never happen. He decided to murder the only three other people who knew about it. Quick and easy. He must have thought he could make some excuse about their disappearance. It was a dangerous expedition, after all, in uncharted territory, among savages. Only something had gone wrong. Rowen was still alive.

Rowen's shoulders drooped slightly, and he gazed down at the earthen floor as he supplied the final bits of the tale.

"Tarnum wanted to control the ship so that he could return alone. He was ignorant of it; a bad mistake. He should have known what would happen when he destroyed Jid. Porix tried to stop him. Porix was brave. But Jid had no defense . . . he could not move . . . the clear glass of his wondrous mind . . . all shattered." Rowen stopped, squeezing his eyes closed as if to shut out the pain of bad memories.

Ruthie stared numbly, trying to get some picture of Jid from Rowen's description. She couldn't make it fit. A mind made of clear glass? It sounded like nonsense. She yearned to ask him more about Jid, but was half afraid.

She remained silent, and after a time Rowen went on. "Without Jid, the craft was not controllable. Tarnum had time for nothing but escape from it. Neither did I. My life lock came to rest near this place. I saw fire beyond the hills. I think that was our ship. I did not know until now whether Tarnum fared well or ill." With that, Rowen fell silent, staring wistfully out at the sagebrush, now a dusty gold in the sunset.

"So you really *are* stranded here—both of you. And you must have been hurt when you landed. Is that what's wrong with you?"

Rowen smiled gravely. "I wish it were that simple. No. Something far greater is wrong with me. I am ill. I am certain that Tarnum is also ill by now, or he would come for me himself instead of sending Tom Castor. It is probable that we will both die soon."

Ruthie was stunned. It couldn't be. He must be mistaken. "But . . . but couldn't a doctor help you? Our doctors know about all kinds of diseases. I could take you to one."

"I would only frighten your doctors. Besides, it would not be good for the secrecy of our mission. People would be alarmed. It is probable that there would be violence. You want to help me, Ruthie Keag. I am grateful. But that is not the way."

"How, then? There must be something. You can't just sit here and die. I don't care what kind of sickness it is, there must be something."

"It is a sickness of those who dwell where they were not meant to dwell. Have you wondered how I am able to breathe this air, drink this water, tolerate the radiations of this star? Can Seldor and your planet be truly so much alike? The probabilities are very, very much against it."

Rowen tapped his chest in the place where Ruthie had seen the metal fitting. "The answer is here," he said. "Earth is a gentle place when seen among other planets. The gravity does not crush me, the atmosphere does not dissolve my body, the heat of this star is almost enough for me. Yet, without this device, I could live no more than a moment on this planet."

"You mean, there's a machine inside you that somehow . . . somehow makes up for the differences between Seldor and Earth?"

"You are correct. It does that by putting certain substances into my body at certain times. But we have been away from Seldor too long now. The substances are almost gone. Some of the substances are not found on Earth, and I have only a few emergency rations. It is possible that Tarnum's rations are also running out."

A lump rose in Ruthie's throat as she realized the seriousness of Rowen's plight. "This is awful," she muttered, running her fingers through her hair. "Have you tried everything? What about the other teams? Maybe you could contact them somehow."

"That is my greatest hope. There is still a group of mapmakers orbiting. But I have not found a way to send them a sign."

He got up from his chair and walked to a table in a dark corner of the room. There he picked up a small box about the size of the wooden match container Ruthie's mother kept by the kitchen stove.

"I now am ashamed," he said. "We did not attend properly to the life locks. Each lock should have one of these. Neither of them did, however." He handed it to her. "It is a communicating device. I thought of taking it as I left the ship. I might have used it to send a message, but it is damaged. My landing was difficult."

Ruthie turned it over, examining it curiously. The device looked simple enough. There were two hemispherical buttons on the outside of it, both of them marked with queer, squiggly symbols—Seldorian writing, she guessed. She shook it gently. It rattled. "Do you know what's wrong with it?" she asked.

"I have not had good fortune in that. I have not discovered the source of the problem."

She was silent for a moment, scrutinizing the box as though, if she looked hard enough, she might see through the cover.

"I know something about electronics—not much, but a little," she said. "Would you let me take this

home with me? I mean, maybe I could figure it out. Maybe I could fix it."

"I would be honored. But you must be careful. There will be great curiosity if it is discovered," Rowen answered.

She nodded. "I know. Don't worry. I'll watch out."

She was suddenly aware that it was dusk. The frogs and crickets by the creek were already in full chorus, and she heard Sundust stamping restlessly outside.

She stood up hurriedly. "Sorry, Rowen. I have to go. I didn't realize it was so late." She was already rushing toward the door, dreading her father's anger.

Rowen followed her outside and watched as she mounted Sundust. "Be careful, my friend. Darkness is coming," he called.

"I will," she answered as she shook the reins. "And you be careful, too."

Rowen put up his hand in a silent salute as she rode away.

The hills were a dark line in the distance, and the sagebrush loomed around her in shadowy billows as she galloped toward the ranch.

It seemed hours before, in a clatter of hooves and a spray of star-frosted pebbles, that Ruthie and Sundust had raced through the gate and up the road to the house. At the sound of horseshoes on gravel, her father appeared on the porch, his weathered face full of worry and anger.

Ruthie dismounted hastily, a huge emptiness in her stomach.

"Dad, I can explain," she blurted. But a second later she realized that she *couldn't* explain. Whatever else she did, she *had* to keep Rowen a secret.

She walked toward the porch, Sundust's reins held loosely in her hand.

"Well, I'm waiting, Ruth," said her father. "Whatever you tell me, it better be the truth."

She knew that if she lied, he'd be able to see it. She wished that she could tell him everything, rely on him to decide what was best. But she couldn't do that either.

She gathered what little courage she could find. "I'm sorry, Dad. I rode out to the foothills and it got dark before I noticed."

He stepped down off the porch and took the reins from her. With his other hand, he grabbed her arm firmly. Ruthie's heart sank. "Do you have any idea how much you worried your mother?"

She was so abashed that she couldn't answer.

He gave her a little shake. "Well?" he demanded. "Did you think about that? Did you think about what happened when dinnertime passed and you didn't come?"

"I'm sorry," she murmured, looking hard at the gray boards of the porch.

"Well you darn well better be. It's just your good luck that I kept your mother from calling Sheriff Thompson."

Ruthie stood without speaking.

"All right," he said, letting go of her arm. "Go in and tell her you're sorry. And one last thing. I don't want to see you riding Sundust for a week. I'll exercise the horse myself. Is that clear?"

"Oh, Dad!" she cried in despair. "A whole week?"

"Git!" he answered.

She felt as if the world had gone out of control and was spinning wildly away to nowhere as she stumbled toward the screen door. How could she possibly help Rowen without Sundust? How could she get to Hidden Creek without her horse?

SEVEN

* * * *

Sabotage

RUTHIE trudged up the stairs to her room, not bothering to turn on the light. She threw herself onto the bed, letting the familiar darkness soothe and comfort her. If only she could explain to her mother and father. She wanted them to be proud of her and of what she was trying to do. She buried her face in the pillow and lay motionless.

It was only a few minutes before she heard footsteps on the stairway. "Are you awake, dear?" It was her mother, silhouetted in the doorway, carrying a tray.

"Yes, Mom," she murmured.

"I brought you some dinner. Thought you might like to eat up here tonight."

"Thanks," Ruthie replied halfheartedly.

Mrs. Keag set the tray on the desk and came over to sit beside Ruthie on the bed.

"Are you all right?" she asked.

"Oh, I guess so," sighed Ruthie, sitting up and curling her arms around her knees.

"You worried us terribly, you know," said Mrs.

Keag. "You've got to learn to keep better track of time."

Ruthie made no reply.

Mrs. Keag shook her head. "You know how your father is, Ruthie. You got him upset. His taking Sundust away shouldn't be a surprise to you."

"Oh, Mom, you don't understand!" said Ruthie, giving way to her misery.

Her mother laughed very softly. She turned her face toward the window. Ruthie could see only her faint, striking profile against the stars. "You might be surprised at how well I understand."

Wordlessly, Ruthie huddled in a tight little ball on the shadowy bed. After a minute or two, her mother got up and walked back to the door.

"Well, good night, dear. Sleep well," she said quietly.

Ruthie ate slowly and without much appetite. Her plate was only half empty when she put it down and crept through the window onto the gently sloping roof of the porch. It was a clear night, stark and beautiful as only the darkness of the desert can be. The Calico Hills rose like great, black animals in the cold radiance of the stars. The immense sky hung above her, strewn with the lights of distant suns. Searching them, she clenched and unclenched her fists. Rowen's small, yellow star was up there somewhere. She felt it should stand out like a blazing nova. But she couldn't even find it among the myriad twinkling lights.

She realized that helping Rowen had become the most important thing in her life. It was no longer just that he fascinated her, or even that he was her friend. It was something far greater than that. She was Earth's ambassador to intelligent beings from the stars! She wished she could run to the crest of the Calicos and shout it out across the plain. Mankind was not alone in the universe, and Rowen was her proof of it.

Ruthie dug in her pocket and pulled out the communicator. The case was smooth and seemed to be cast all in one piece. She could feel no seams, no screws or rivets. She wondered how much alike the logic of humans and Seldorians could be. Common sense dictated that there was a way to open the case for repairs. But that was the common sense of someone born and raised on Earth. Feeling tired and unsure of herself, Ruthie rested her chin on her knees and looked sadly out across the flats.

Ruthie awoke in the gray of dawn, before the sun had come up over the hills. Refreshed by a night's sleep, she dressed quickly in the morning chill. Urgency filled her to bursting. Shivering, she wondered whether Rowen, too, had slept well. When she thought of him now, he seemed thinner and older than he had before, practically fading before her eyes. If only a few bits of good luck would come their way. Determined to succeed, she sat down at her desk with her box of tools and the communicator.

Ruthie tried everything she could think of to open the case. She poked and jiggled, hoping at first that she might find some hidden latch or fastener. When that failed, she tried repeatedly to slip her screwdriver under the little rim where the control buttons came up. But when she examined the area with a magnifying glass, she discovered that the buttons and the case were somehow melded in an even, seamless surface. She had just begun to try a small hacksaw blade on the communicator when she heard her mother calling her for breakfast. Hurriedly, she opened the desk drawer and piled everything in, shutting it with a frustrated bang.

She rushed through breakfast and asked to be excused five minutes after she'd sat down. Her father eyed her coldly, then gave mute permission, jerking his head in the direction of the door. She could still feel his anger like heat from a smoldering fire.

She bounded up the stairs, anxious to get back to work and glad to escape that reproving gaze. Slipping into her chair once more, she tugged open the desk drawer. Gazing down into it, she was puzzled. She distinctly remembered having flung the communicator into the drawer before going down to breakfast. But the familiar black box was no longer there. Dismayed, she took a closer look. In place of the communicator was an unfamiliar object, something that looked like a mass of red, metallic worms.

With a start, Ruthie realized that she was looking at the inside of Rowen's communicator. The back half of the case was gone! Eagerly, she lifted the communicator out of the drawer. But as soon as she had it in her hands, the case materialized before her eyes. She was so startled that she almost dropped it. She felt as if she were watching an eerie magic show.

Holding the communicator in the sun, Ruthie turned it over and over, staring at it in amazement. What could have made the case disappear? She wondered what she could be overlooking. She squinted at the case. It gleamed brightly in the morning light. But she noticed one spot on the back that shone even more brightly than the rest. Examining it more closely, she found that the small, disk-shaped area seemed to be made of a different material. She pulled her screwdriver out of the drawer and poked at the spot. As if she had worked a miracle, the back half of the case shimmered, became translucent, then disappeared entirely! With a little gasp of astonishment, she leaned over for a closer look. But as soon as she did so, the case reappeared.

"What did I do?" she muttered aloud. Then she realized that in her excitement, she had moved the screwdriver away from the strange spot. When she put the tool back, the case disappeared again.

Taking care not to move the screwdriver, Ruthie gazed at the alien interior of the communicator. She recognized none of the components, though their arrangement seemed hauntingly familiar. The foil tracks that connect components on a standard Earth-made circuit board were missing altogether. In their place were the wide, wriggly, red lines that looked so much like worms.

It was awkward using one hand to hold the screwdriver down on the spot. Ruthie lifted the screwdriver once more, and as she expected, the case reappeared. What was it about this particular tool that made the case disappear? She now remembered that the screwdriver had been lying on the communicator when she first opened the drawer as well. She tried touching the disk-shaped area with a pencil. Nothing happened, perhaps because the pencil wasn't metal. But she tried several metal objects—a safety pin, a piece of bailing wire, and an old nail. None of them had any effect.

Puzzled and exasperated, she pushed back her chair and stood up, taking the screwdriver into her hands, holding its heavy handle while she tried to think. It was quite an ordinary screwdriver with a long, steel blade and a yellow plastic grip. Yet other objects made of the same materials had no effect on the case. What was she missing?

Ruthie scooped up the safety pin and the wire. Yes, they were certainly made of steel. She held everything in one hand while she rummaged in her pocket for other objects she could try. There were a quartz pebble, three pennies, and some rubber bands. She tossed them onto the desk along with the items from her other hand. Then, gazing at the odd array before her, she realized something that almost made her shout with excitement. The safety pin and the bailing wire, both steel, were stuck to the blade of the screwdriver. She had forgotten that it was magnetized!

Feverishly, she ransacked the desk drawers until she found the small, cube-shaped magnet that she had won in a marble game the previous spring. She set it down on the disk. The case disappeared immediately. Unable to contain herself any longer, Ruthie leaped up and gave a whoop of joy.

But it took only a moment for her to realize how silly it was to rejoice. True, she had managed to open the case and could now see the intricate circuitry that lay within. But her success so far had been blind luck. The job ahead of her, diagnosing the still-unknown defect and repairing it, would take hard work, careful thought, and plenty of additional good luck.

Ruthie raced downstairs to telephone Kate McGee. She wanted to have a few reference books from the library before she really began. She could trust Kate to bring the books, and she knew her friend would waste no time. Kate would understand how important this was.

* * *

That afternoon, Ruthie was waiting by the gate at the end of the ranch road when Kate galloped up.

"How've you been?" cried Kate, reaching down to grab Ruthie's arm and help her into the saddle.

"Oh, okay," Ruthie answered with a small grin. "Did you get the books?"

"I sure did, easy as pie. Only they didn't have very many. I even got Mrs. Dangberg, that nice new librarian, to help me. But we only found three."

"That's okay," said Ruthie as they rode toward the house. "I knew they didn't have a lot of new books on electronics. I'm just happy you did me the favor. It's really important to me, Kate."

"Well, I don't mind a bit. It's fun to come out and see you. The ride is kind of nice, and Pearly likes it, too." She stroked the horse's dusty neck.

When they got to the house, the girls dismounted and Kate tied Pearl to the porch rail. Eagerly, Ruthie opened the saddlebags and pulled out the books.

"Ruthie, what's this all about? What are we going to do with these?" Kate picked up two heavy volumes bound in red. "*A Primer of Chip Technology. Modern Integrated Circuitry.* Boy, these look pretty complicated."

"I hope it's not *too* tough," Ruthie replied, examining a copy of *Principles of the Semiconductor.*

Kate looked at her worriedly. "All right, Ruthie," she said in a low voice. "Tell me what's happened. You know we're in this together. Does it have something to do with Tom and that strange guy?"

Ruthie pursed her lips. She stared out across the brush where heat waves shimmered like water in the distance. After a long moment, she made up her mind. "I think it's time to tell you the whole story, Kate. I

73

would have let you in on it sooner, but I was afraid. I just couldn't."

Kate stared silently, her blue eyes very wide, as Ruthie tried to decide where to begin the strange tale.

"Look, Kate. You've got to promise to keep this a secret," said Ruthie.

Sparks of excitement lit up Kate's eyes. "I can keep a secret," she whispered.

Ruthie took a deep breath. "I hope you'll believe me. On my honor, this is the truth, no matter how strange it sounds. It all started with that old man I found at Hidden Creek."

Slowly and quietly, Ruthie told Kate the long, complex tale of Rowen and Tarnum and the series of events that had left them stranded on a planet that was slowly killing them. She explained how kind and brave Rowen was, and how Tarnum wanted to get rid of him to avoid the consequences of a scandal on Seldor.

At last, she explained why she'd asked Kate to go to the library for her. "I had to have the books to find out about Rowen's communicator, but I couldn't get to town without Sundust. I still don't know how I'm going to get back to Hidden Creek, even if I *do* manage to fix the communicator."

"Don't worry, Ruthie. Pearl and I will help any way we can. This is important. Why, it's life and death!"

Ruthie was about to thank Kate when she heard an odd noise on the porch roof above them. "What's that?"

Kate cocked her head, listening. "I don't know. Is someone up on the roof?"

Before Ruthie could reply, there was a dull thud, and a cloud of dust rose in front of them. Too startled to move, the girls watched as a lean, red-haired figure darted away across the yard.

It was Tom Castor, and in his hand he carried a small, black object. Ruthie shouted in panic, "It's the communicator! He's got the communicator!"

Both girls sprinted after Tom as he ran down the road. To their dismay, he sped toward a big clump of sage brush and wheeled his motorcycle out of hiding. By the time they caught up with him, he already had the engine started.

"Stop!" cried Ruthie hoarsely.

"Don't worry. I'll catch him!" shouted Kate, racing back to the porch and vaulting into Pearl's saddle like an Olympic athlete.

"Don't! It's too dangerous!" screamed Ruthie, but it was too late. Headstrong Kate was already galloping full speed down the road after Tom.

Ruthie watched in disbelief as Tom suddenly swerved sideways in a shower of gravel, purposely blocking the road as Kate and Pearl rushed toward him. He shouted a name in the direction of a near-by stand of cottonwoods. Kate was nearly upon him, reining Pearl in for an emergency stop, when someone sprang from the cottonwoods into the road in front of her. There was no mistaking Tarnum, his face brick-red under an ill-fitting knit cap. Dancing with glee, Tarnum grabbed clumsily at the communicator in Tom's hand. Watching helplessly, Ruthie shrieked as she saw the case slip and smash to the ground in front of the horse.

Pearl's eyes rolled with fright as she dug her front legs into the sandy earth and put her head down. Kate hurtled over the horse's neck, somersaulting in mid-air. Then a swirling cloud of dust and the frantic roar of the motorbike's engine tore the stillness of the desert asunder.

EIGHT

* * * *

Furtive
Departure

B Y the time Ruthie reached Kate, Tom and Tarnum
were far down the road, racing toward Sand Fork.
The desert insects and birds had fallen strangely silent; the only sound was of Kate spitting grit from her
mouth as she emerged from the dust, looking like a dis-
concerted ghost.

Ruthie waved her arms to clear the air. "Kate!
Kate!" she yelled. "Are you okay?"

"I . . . I hurt my arm." Kate spat again, and peered
in confusion from eyes that seemed supernaturally
bright against her soiled face.

Ruthie looked at her friend in alarm. Kate stood before her, weaving slightly, her shoulders hunched forward. There was no blood, but her right arm hung crook-
edly at her side. "Can you move it?" asked Ruthie.

"Ow . . . it hurts!" she gasped, wincing as she tried
to lift it.

A sudden rivulet of sweat ran down Kate's forehead, exposing a swath of skin too pale for comfort. "I think we better get you to the house," said Ruthie, bending to position herself under Kate's good arm. "I think it must be broken. It doesn't look so hot."

"Yeah . . . it kind of hurts," Kate replied, panting, as they hurried toward the ranch house. Ruthie could tell from her face that the pain was worse than she'd admitted. Though Kate did not make a sound, two tears began to creep down her cheeks.

"Just lean on me, and don't worry," said Ruthie, smiling, trying valiantly to keep her own voice from quavering. "Hey—I bet you'll get a cast. And everybody in Sand Fork will come and help you decorate it."

"Yeah. I hadn't thought of that," said Kate, grinning lopsidedly through her tears.

By now, Ruthie could see her mother running down the road toward them calling, "Is she all right?"

"We think her arm's broken," Ruthie called.

When Mrs. Keag reached them, Ruthie said, "I'll go get Dad to bring the jeep around, okay?"

"Fine . . . fine, dear. Katie and I can get to the house all right, can't we?"

Ruthie loped back toward Pearl, who stood motionless a few yards from the gate, her head held low, reins dragging in the dust. Her terror had vanished along with Tom's motorcycle.

Ruthie leaped into Pearl's saddle and started toward the northwest field at a gallop. How could Tom and Tarnum have been so incredibly stupid? Kate had been very lucky. She might easily have been killed in a fall such as that. Ruthie could hardly believe the recent change in Tom Castor. He knew horses. He must have been aware of the foolhardiness of his actions. Nevertheless, he'd deliberately spooked Kate's horse. Had

78

Tarnum instigated it? And even if he had, how could he possibly exert such power over Tom? The memory of Rowen's communicator lying smashed in the roadway filled her with almost uncontrollable fury. Smart move, Tarnum, she thought, cracking the reins recklessly. Now neither of them had one chance in a billion of getting help from Seldor in time. Tarnum must be the greatest idiot in the galaxy!

With a twinge of guilt, Ruthie realized that in her anger she'd been driving Pearl much harder than was necessary. She was rapidly approaching the west fence, where her father stood digging a posthole. As she drew closer, she saw him throw down his shovel, pause for an instant as if frozen, and throw himself into the driver's seat of the jeep. He sped toward her, raising a powdery cloud from the spinning tires. Something in the way Ruthie pushed the unfamiliar horse must have warned him of trouble.

Braking hard, he skidded to a stop. Ruthie catapulted down from the saddle and sprang into the seat beside him. "What's the matter?" he yelled above the noisy engine.

"It's Kate McGee," said Ruthie breathlessly. "She broke her arm. Horse threw her. Out by our gate."

Mr. Keag needed no further information. Gunning the reliable old jeep, he zoomed back toward the house, leaving Pearl alone in the field to find her own way home.

Ruthie pulled the brush briskly across Pearl's sweat-glistening back, her anger and frustration adding to the vigor of her motions. In the quiet, cool atmosphere of the barn, she found it hard to accept the cruel events of the afternoon. But in her pocket the shattered fragments of Rowen's communicator rattled in grim confirmation.

She had felt so small and helpless trying to comfort Kate as she lay on the sofa while Mr. Keag telephoned the doctor in Sand Fork. For the first time, she was deeply frightened of Tarnum, and she began to wonder whether she'd gotten herself into a no-win situation.

While Mrs. Keag got some aspirin for Kate, Ruthie helped her father make a bed of soft straw and blankets in the back of the jeep. Then he and her mother and Kate hurried away toward town, leaving Ruthie alone to bring Pearl home and stable her.

Now, in the barn, she brushed Pearl harder and faster than ever. "I hope they find those two and put them away forever!" she cried aloud. "It's one thing to take the communicator and wreck it, but for what they did to Kate, they ought to be put in jail and never let out!"

In his stall nearby, Sundust whinnied softly as he munched on a scoopful of oats. "I wish I were you, Sundust," said Ruthie. "I wish everything were simple, and people treated each other as well as they treat their horses!"

Her parents had still not returned by the time she had finished Pearl's thorough grooming session. For a while Ruthie paced back and forth in front of the barn, waiting for the plume of dust that would signal a car coming down the road. But after half an hour she grew tired of pacing. Resigned to a longer wait than she had hoped, Ruthie threw herself down on a pile of straw.

The next thing she knew, someone's hand was on her shoulder gently shaking her awake. She must have dozed off.

"Come on, Ruth. Wake up. Your mother's gettin' supper."

"Dad," she mumbled groggily, sitting up and rubbing her sleepy eyes. All at once, the day's events rushed back to her. "Dad! You're back! How's Kate?" she cried.

"She'll be okay. Don't worry." He smiled, and his furrowed, somber face grew gentle. "We had to take her to the hospital in Paleyville. That's what took us so long. But she'll be fine."

"Paleyville!" Ruthie exclaimed. "But that's so far away. How long will she be there?"

"Oh, a few days, I guess. They're being extra careful. If it doesn't heal right, they might have to operate later to put in a metal pin. But with a little luck, she'll be fine without that."

"I hope they catch Tom," Ruthie fumed. "I hope they send him to a reformatory."

Mr. Keag shook his head. "Kate's folks don't want to press charges against him. It's that other fellow, the stranger. He's the one we're all wondering about. Nobody's ever seen him before." He shook his head and continued, "Sheriff Thompson is looking for them, but nobody knows where they've disappeared to."

Ruthie swallowed hard. She hadn't thought about it until now, but things would be worse than ever if the sheriff found Tarnum. She was certain that Tarnum would immediately tell the authorities the location of Rowen's hiding place. And who knows what stories he might invent to save his own skin and place the blame on Rowen. She kept these thoughts to herself as she sat, suddenly uncomfortable in the heap of straw.

Mr. Keag gazed at her quizzically. "I can't figure out what's the matter with that young Tom. He's always had his troubles, but this mean streak is different."

Ruthie rested her head on her knees silently, afraid to reply.

Her father traced designs in the dusty earth with the tip of his finger. "What's going on between you two? He's got some kind of a grudge against you. It's plain to see."

Ruthie squeezed her lips tightly together. A noncommittal shrug was her only answer.

She saw her father's jaw harden in displeasure. "Sometimes I just can't understand you," he said. "As far as I'm concerned, nothing could be worth what happened to Kate today. Whatever this is all about, it's got to stop. It's time to make amends when people start getting hurt, and that's all there is to it."

Ruthie hunched wordlessly in the straw, afraid that speaking might loose the flood of apprehension and distress that she fought to hold back.

There was a long pause. She knew he was waiting for some explanation, some sentence that would neatly reveal the central problem. But she held stubbornly to her silence.

Her father rose to his feet, looking the way he sometimes did when coyotes got into the chicken coop or thunderstorms washed away the fences. "Well, I'll be dadblamed if I'm gonna sit around here and try to teach you the good sense you shoulda been born with. Better come and eat." He turned and walked away into the summer dusk. Gazing after him, she realized that she would never get him to let her ride Sundust now. Her only choice was to go to Hidden Creek behind her father's back. It was either that or let Rowen die.

As soon as dinner was over, Ruthie went to her bedroom and shut the door loudly behind her. She took off her boots and tied them together, running a piece of thick twine through the straps. Quietly, she opened her closet and gathered a few articles of warm clothing and a flashlight, stuffing them into her kit. She slipped a watertight container of matches and a box of cartridges for her rifle into her shirt pocket. Finally, she reached for her bedroll, a sturdily made down sleeping bag, lightweight and warm.

As a last precaution, she took the pillows from her bed and bunched them up beneath the blankets. Anyone looking into the darkened room might assume she was sleeping. The trick might very well buy her some extra time.

Ruthie put on her hat and hung her boots and saddlebags over her shoulder. After making sure her rifle was empty, the bolt back, and the safety catch engaged, she carefully tied it to her sleeping bag and slipped a long rope through the pack ties. Then, stealthily, she crawled through the window and out onto the porch roof. It was an easy matter to lower the bag quietly to the ground. And it wasn't very hard to shinny down the post into the yard. She had done it many times before, though never as quietly or as carefully. Now, past practice served her well.

She padded across the yard in her stocking feet, keeping to the shadows, holding her breath for fear of discovery. Soon she was standing before the heavy wooden door that led to the root cellar. By the slender beam of her flashlight, she raised the door and crept down the stairs. Hurriedly, she shoved tins of beans, stew, tomatoes, and other canned goods into every empty space she could find in her saddlebags.

A few minutes later, she groped through the warm

darkness of the barn, the familiar smells of hay, alfalfa pellets, and animal dung surrounding her like a feather comforter.

"Sundust!" she called softly as she untied her boots and pulled them on. "How about a little ride?"

There was an answering whinny from his stall.

Ruthie pulled the bridle from its peg on the wall. She could have saddled Sundust even if she'd been struck blind. She knew every ripple of his great back, and she knew the saddle itself like an old and trusty friend. She had often readied her horse for riding before the dawn, in that black, waiting hour when the birds begin to stir expectantly, and the night creatures have silently retired. She needed no light for that. With sure hands, she buckled the bridle, threw on the thick blanket, and lifted the saddle into place, cinching it expertly.

No one heard them as they walked down the road through the gate—no one but Farmer, who whined softly, then tagged along beside them.

NINE

* * * *

Attack in
the Dark

RUTHIE urged Sundust as quickly as he would go along the dim trail to Hidden Creek. The path was well worn, and she stuck to it carefully, knowing that his fresh hoofprints would blend with the old ones and might not be noticed. Her father would soon be looking for her, perhaps even before dawn, and she didn't intend to be discovered. The moon was a fragile sliver in the deep, star-decked sky, offering no light to comfort her. Tonight the desert was a black and forbidding place.

It seemed forever before the warm, yellow light in the window of the miner's shack twinkled invitingly in the distance. She was glad to be approaching the safety of Rowen's house. After dark, strange animals came out to hunt, and their unfamiliar cries left her feeling edgy.

Sundust trotted up to the hitching post, and Ruthie dismounted quickly. Rowen met her at the door, smiling, the *Webster's* dictionary open in his hands.

"Sorry to interrupt, Rowen. Could I come in?" she asked softly.

"Of course, my friend. Please. You must come in. There is no interruption." He swung the door wide for her and ushered her inside.

"I did not expect to see you now," he went on. "I thought that humans slept whenever the sun was not in the sky."

"Well, we usually do. But there's no way I could sleep tonight. There's all kinds of trouble. I had to come over right away. It couldn't wait till morning. I hope it's okay."

The smile faded from his face as Ruthie's agitation became clear. "Please come in. I am always glad to see you."

Clutching her wide-brimmed hat, Ruthie shuffled into the room. "Something awful's happened. It's Tarnum again," she said, ill at ease and too warm in the heat from the old wood stove.

"What has he done?"

"I can still hardly believe it. He . . . he and Tom Castor came out to the ranch this afternoon and stole the communicator. They smashed it to bits. And when my friend Kate McGee tried to stop them, they spooked her horse. She fell and broke her arm." The words rushed out, tumbling over one another like rocks in a landslide. "Rowen, your chances of getting out of this are ruined. I don't know what to do."

She realized that she was crying. Through her tears, she was aware of Rowen's hand on her arm, guiding her to a chair. As if in a dream, she heard his soothing voice as he spoke to her in what must have been Seldorian. She thought of her Grandfather Peterson who, in his youth, had come from Denmark on a sailing

86

ship to seek his fortune as a silver miner on the Comstock Lode. Long ago, she had gone to him with her deepest fears and troubles. He was as constant as the west wind, unflappable, full of wisdom. He often spoke to her in Danish. Curled on his warm and ample lap, the meaning of the words seemed unimportant. They had always calmed her without fail, as Rowen's did now.

As she wiped her eyes roughly on the sleeve of her shirt, Rowen said, "Do not despair, my friend. Worse troubles than these I have seen in my life. Always I have sought the joy of adventure. But the partner of adventure is trouble. These things I understand."

"Worse trouble than this?"

Rowen smiled and shrugged. "The ice creatures of Fornax, the ammonia bogs of Regulus Five, even the predator clouds of deep space—all were fiercer enemies than Tarnum. I remain not defeated. I have devised a plan."

"You have?" Ruthie sniffed, brightening.

"Perhaps it will not work. Still, it offers me some chance. I propose to find the wreck of our ship. I know which way to travel. When I entered the life lock, I had in my pocket an instrument for locating metal objects. It can help me now. And perhaps I will find a communicator in the wreckage."

"Rowen! That's exactly what *I* was thinking. It's a terrific idea!" exclaimed Ruthie. "But you *can't* go alone. It's too dangerous, and you're sick. I want to come, too. Will you let me, please?"

"I do not ask you to come, my friend. The difficulties will be great."

"I know," said Ruthie, hanging her head. "But . . . I didn't tell you the whole story. You see, I ran away from home tonight. I had to. It was the only way I could get out to tell you what happened. There wasn't enough time. I couldn't wait. Anyway, we've gotta get out of here. This is the first place they'll look for me. Let me come with you, Rowen. We can ride Sundust. It's the only thing to do!"

"It is clear in your mind?"

"Absolutely."

Rowen got slowly to his feet. "Are we to go now, and not wait for the sun to rise?"

Ruthie gazed out at the cold, lightless sky, imagining a journey in the hazards of darkness. But the best path was clear. "Yes, now," she replied.

While Rowen gathered some essentials, Ruthie took Sundust and Farmer down to the creek. She got out the canteens and the water bags. She didn't know quite where they would be going, but she knew better than to trust the desert for water.

"Drink up, boys," she murmured as the canteens gurgled in the dark, icy stream. Contemplating the black hills that rose in shadow beyond the cottonwoods, Ruthie prayed that the desert would treat them kindly.

Within minutes, Ruthie was helping Rowen up into Sundust's saddle. "Which way do we go?" she asked, as she checked to make sure that their provisions and equipment were well anchored for the journey.

"To the other side of the hills," he answered. "Let us go quickly."

Jumping up behind Rowen, Ruthie held the reins loosely in front of him, encircling him with her arms. No doubt he had never been on a horse before. That was enough of a handicap. But when coupled with his illness, the result might easily be exhaustion. She could not risk his falling from the saddle.

She gazed upstream toward the shadowy cleft where Hidden Creek disappeared into the Calico Hills. "Let's go up the streambed. We'll be harder to track that way," she said.

"Good," he replied, glancing down the dark trail toward the ranch. "Again I say let us go quickly. There are people nearby. I hear them."

"Where?" exclaimed Ruthie, with a sinking feeling. Surely her parents hadn't already discovered she was missing. She cocked her head, straining to hear the telltale cracking of twigs above the steady rush of the creek.

"They are coming down this road." His voice held a quiet urgency that sent fear spurting through her veins.

Ruthie didn't wait another second. "Come on, boy," she cried softly in Sundust's ear. And the horse responded without hesitation, stepping into the cold water of the stream. Quickly and steadily he carried them away from the glade and up into the forbidding barrenness of the Calico Hills. Farmer trotted behind, picking his way along the stream bank.

When the miner's shack was far behind, Ruthie guided Sundust back up onto the bank. The danger of immediate discovery was past, and the bank offered surer footing.

Ruthie was the first to break the silence that had hung between her and Rowen since leaving the shack. "Could you tell who was coming?" She was thinking of her first conversation with him, and of how he had "remembered her sounds."

"I could not tell. They were too far away." Rowen shifted uncomfortably in the saddle. "There was more than one creature, walking on two legs. Perhaps it was Tom Castor and Tarnum."

"Or a search party," Ruthie whispered.

They followed the stream bank as closely as they could until at last, when the slender moon was far up in the sky, they found a safe camping place in a grassy clearing near some poplar trees. After helping Rowen climb out of the saddle, Ruthie went about setting up camp. The campsite would be at the center of the clearing where intruders would have difficulty sneaking up on them.

Ruthie rolled out their bedding and trotted off in search of firewood. Soon she and Rowen were wrapped in blankets, warming their hands in the heat of a dancing flame. Overhead, the stars hung in the desert sky like chains dripping with diamonds.

"Can you show me Seldor?" asked Ruthie.

Rowen sat up among his blankets. "Do you know the constellations?" he asked.

"Steve Washoe taught me some of them. But there are still a lot that I don't always recognize," she admitted.

"I have great interest in your constellations," he said, smiling. "In all the galaxy, no other race of beings has seen pictures in the stars. In many ways, human-kind is unique."

In a voice as soft as moonlight he continued, "You must learn of the stars, for among them your future lies. You must come to know them as you know old friends."

"Up there?" Ruthie stared into the spattered sky as if she were seeing it for the first time. There lay a land of adventure and danger, a home for pioneers, a high-way for travelers. Against that awesome backdrop, the troubles of Earth shrank to nothing, and seemed of little importance.

"Look south," said Rowen, pointing. "Through that low place in the hills is a star of great brightness, sailing low, almost among the trees."

"Yes!" cried Ruthie in excitement. "I see it."

"That is the star known to you as Antares. West of Antares and somewhat higher are two more stars, not of such brightness."

"Okay—I see them."

"Seldor orbits the higher of those two stars."

For a while, they watched Rowen's sun in silence. Ruthie strained to see some clue, some trace of Seldor whirling about the tiny light. But there was none. Only her newfound knowledge set this star apart from its countless neighbors.

"What's Seldor like?" she asked.

From Rowen's lips came a delicate sound, like a crystal wind chime or the jingling that stars might make on a frosty night if they could speak to one another. It was almost soft laughter, almost a song.

"The mountains of Seldor are high. On their stony peaks always the sky is black, the view of stars unspoiled. The canyons are deep, so deep that the heart of Seldor seethes like a river in the abyss. But also there are hills where grass grows the color of a star in its red gianthood. There are valley trees, with leaves that gleam like gemstones. There are lakes of quicksilver, cities of bronze. There are creatures of many sizes—little *bexen* that hide in the crimson grasses, great *meraps* that sweep through the air like swift clouds.

"I live far from any city, beside a brook that runs with water made sweet by the roots of *shindakoo* plants. Leral shares my dwelling, my food, my books.

91

When I am far from home, I think of her near the water. I think of the sunlight on her cheeks. Much time ago, when we were young, I found Leral by the water, and we made the compact that means friendship, but more than friendship."

Ruthie grinned. "She's your wife, isn't she?"

"I have not found the exact word in the tongues of Earth. 'Wife' is almost right." Rowen looked up into the sky. "I am sad to be so long away from Seldor. I am sadder still to be so long away from Leral."

Ruthie broke a twig and threw it into the fire. The thought of Leral bravely waiting for someone who might never come home was almost more than she could stand.

"Do you have any children?" she asked quietly.

"We are old. The little ones much time ago grew up and went away," he replied.

There wouldn't even be any children to comfort Leral. Blindly casting about for some bit of reassurance, Ruthie said with as much confidence as she could muster, "Don't worry, Rowen. You'll get home somehow, in spite of Tarnum, in spite of everything!"

All at once, the perfection of the desert night was shattered as Farmer scrambled to his feet, barking and showing his teeth, the hair on his back erect.

Ruthie grabbed the rifle and stumbled out of her bedroll in alarm. She thought she saw a low, moving shape on the edge of the clearing. A second later, she heard the unmistakable snapping of twigs as someone or something moved through the undergrowth. Farmer dashed forward, snarling like a wolf. Ruthie started after him, but stopped when the sudden pain of a sharp stone reminded her that she'd taken off her boots.

She stood tautly, not knowing what to do, until a

piercing shriek and a series of agonized yelps reached her across the blackness. "Farmer!" she shouted. She laid down the rifle and ran back for her boots.

But by the time she had them on, Farmer was limping back toward the fire, whining, his tail between his legs. "Oh, Farmer!" she cried, and threw her arms around his neck. There was an ugly gash on one of his forepaws.

Rowen was on his feet, too, by then. After looking at Farmer's paw, he frowned. "That was not made by teeth. Not all of the cries we heard were Farmer's, I am certain," he said. "The intruder did not escape unharmed."

Ruthie shivered. "Who do you think it was?"

Rowen replied gravely, "It was Tarnum."

TEN

* * * *

Jid

RUTHIE rose eagerly as the early morning light began to bleach the stars from the sky. She had slept very little; frightening images of Tarnum defending himself against Farmer kept her awake far into the night. But the heavy fatigue of the previous day was gone, and as the sky steadily brightened, she went about fixing a light breakfast.

By the time Rowen awoke, the first rays of sun reached into the clearing and Ruthie had breakfast ready to serve. Rowen munched the biscuit Ruthie gave him while she began to gather up their gear.

"Will much time pass before we reach the top of these hills?" he asked, squinting into the distance.

"Naw—just a couple of hours at the most," answered Ruthie, anxiously noting that he looked as if he hadn't slept very well.

"Will we rest there?"

"Sure. We can rest anytime you want to. Just let me know."

"I will," Rowen replied, finishing his biscuit. Then,

placing his foot on a stirrup, he mounted Sundust a little clumsily but without help.

They rode along in silence for a time. Here and there they passed the small tributaries of Hidden Creek, most of them fed by underground springs. Ruthie knew that soon the easy part of their journey would be over. When they could no longer ride beside the creek, they would have to rely on what they could carry with them. Sundust would have no more grass to chew on, and they would have to make do with the water in the canteens.

By mid-morning, they stood beside a rugged outcropping of rock where a spring bubbled from the ground and rushed away down the hillside.

"Well, this is where Hidden Creek begins. Which way now?" asked Ruthie.

"We must climb up to that high place," answered Rowen, pointing to where a long ridge of bedrock stood out against the vivid blue of the sky.

Ruthie dismounted and led Sundust slowly upward, allowing him to find his own path among the sharp and crumbly rocks. Rowen stayed in the saddle, holding fast to the horn. She'd been watching him closely, knowing how strenuous the ride must be for him. He'd been very quiet all morning, and she was worried.

At the top of the ridge, a strong, hot wind greeted them from the east like the ominous breath of a lion. Ruthie fancied they could see to the end of the world. A great plain spread out before them, flat except for a few dark and lonely hills. At the distant horizon, earth and sky met in a fuzzy band made reddish by the dust of the desert. There were no towns, no trees, no ranches. She knew very well that there was nothing but harsh, dry wilderness to the east for hundreds of miles. But she also knew that searchers looking for her would only go east of the Calicos as a last resort. She and Rowen would find, amid the perils of desert travel, a kind of safety there—as long as Tarnum and Tom Castor did not follow them.

From his vantage point on Sundust's back, Rowen stared silently out across the flats where the only motion was a solitary, moaning dust devil. Despite the heat, he was shivering, and his face had gone pale.

"Rowen, are you okay?" Ruthie asked, taking a step toward him.

He didn't answer.

She repeated it a bit louder, softly touching his leg. "Rowen, are you okay?"

The hot wind ruffled his short, white hair and tossed the folds of his iridescent robe in shining waves.

"I am cold," he said at last.

Ruthie was suddenly frightened. The wind howled out of the east like a blast furnace, sucking the moisture from her hands and her face. It was anything but cold.

"Let me get you a blanket," she said.

"Many thanks." He laid a thin hand on her shoulder. "There is a good blanket in my bag. You will see it on top."

As quickly as she could, she undid the strange fastenings of Rowen's bag and found the blanket. It was shiny like his robe, and made of such a lightweight material that she didn't understand how it could be of much use. Nevertheless, she stood on the stirrup and wrapped him up like an Eskimo.

"Better?" she asked anxiously.

"Very much," he replied with a wan smile. "I am once more in your debt."

Working one of his hands free of the blanket, he showed Ruthie a small, thin disk of what looked like colored glass. "This is the metal locating device of which I spoke," he said.

Straightening his arm in front of him, he began to sweep the horizon. At a point northeast of them on the plain, the little disk began to hum. Rowen tried it again, with identical results.

"Do you see the three hills together?" he asked, looking over at her. "The ones with the crown of rocks?"

She picked them out easily. They were a remarkable group, not more than five or six miles away. She had seen them before. They were known in Sand Fork as "The Dutchman's Ladies." An unwelcome thought skittered into her mind. There was supposed to be an abandoned silver mine somewhere among the Dutchman's Ladies.

"Rowen, are you pretty sure you saw the ship come down in this direction?"

"Yes. Quite certain."

"Well, there might be a silver deposit in those three hills. Would that throw your reading off?"

"It is possible," said Rowen, frowning at this development. "However, there is no strong response from another direction."

He paused for a moment, then looked at her and said, "My friend, I have not much to lose by traveling to those hills."

That was true enough, Ruthie thought. Staying where they were was almost the same as surrendering to the sheriff. "Well, okay. Let's rest awhile, though. You look like you could use it. We can be down there in

98

no time. An hour—maybe two. We could camp there to-night. Make a fire, fix a hot meal."

But Rowen surprised her by replying, "No. No rest yet. Someone is not far behind us. We will be discovered."

Ruthie glanced uneasily over her shoulder. Catching Sundust's reins, she took the lead on foot, starting down the unfriendly eastern slope of the Calicos as quickly as she could.

Their progress was not as smooth as she had hoped. Although she urged Sundust along as fast as he would go, sharp stones and jagged outcroppings of basalt forced them to make many detours.

When they finally reached the flats, Ruthie mounted up again behind Rowen and put Sundust into a trot. Nothing blocked their way now except rabbitholes and clumps of sage. But they were far more vulnerable than they had been on any other part of their trip, for there was no way to hide on the plain. From the ridge, they would be readily visible as the only moving objects in miles. The closest shelter was the Dutchman's Ladies themselves.

By midafternoon, when they finally reached the first of the hills, they were tired. Rowen dozed fitfully in the saddle. Farmer lagged far behind, limping along on his three good paws.

A gully where two of the hills came together led them unexpectedly into a little valley. On their way across the flats, with fatigue creeping inexorably into her bones, Ruthie had decided not to get her hopes up about what they might find among the Dutchman's Ladies. Shelter in the abandoned mine was the only expectation she'd allowed herself.

Looking across the valley now, it took her a moment

to realize that their greatest hopes had been fulfilled. They had found the ship.

Pieces of it were spread across the entire floor of the hollow. There was no way of telling the original shape of the craft, or even how large it had been. But every twisted remnant filled her with wonder. Before her lay the bits and pieces of a technology that human beings might never comprehend. Before her was a miracle from another star, single-handedly laid waste by Tarnum's all-consuming ambitions.

Judging from the looks of the wreckage, it was going to be all but impossible to find a communicator in working order. That thought, combined with the weariness that clung to her, made it almost impossible to hold back tears. "Rowen, I'm sorry this happened to you. We could have made it so much easier for you, if only human beings weren't so silly and so afraid of things."

Rowen swung stiffly down from Sundust's back and put his arm around her shoulders. "It is done. It cannot be undone, my friend. And concerning humans, I know of one who is as fine as any being in all the galaxy," he said gently. "Do not be sad. Something here will perhaps be of use to us."

Ruthie gazed at his thin body through a haze of tears. She wondered how long it would be before the little pump inside him stopped working altogether. Almost frantically she forced the thought out of her mind. She wouldn't waste time brooding about it—not now, not ever.

The inviting idea of pitching camp after their long journey gave Ruthie new strength and determination. A few minutes of exploration revealed the legendary silver mine to be nothing more than a pile of tailings beside a shaft that had long since caved in. They found a more suitable campsite in a sheltered triangular clearing, flanked on two sides by boulders. There they unpacked, and Ruthie removed Sundust's saddle and bridle, allowing him to wander about the hillsides searching for anything he might find to eat. She gave Rowen the canteen, then took a short drink herself.

"There's still quite a bit of daylight left," she said, surveying the wreckage of the ship. "I'd like to look around before dinner."

"I will accompany you," Rowen insisted. Then, anticipating her objections, he added, "I know where the communicators were before the crash. It will be helpful."

Leaving Farmer behind to guard the camp, Ruthie followed Rowen, her arms out for balance as they picked their way through a hole in a bulkhead. Carefully, she came along behind him, wondering about everything she saw, awestruck at how little of it she understood. There was an eerie feeling in the valley, as if the hills themselves remembered the horror of the crash. She was tense and jumpy. The place felt haunted.

"Rowen?" she called, hesitating at the dark edge of the ragged opening through which he had gone. "Are you in there?"

"I am here," he answered, his voice echoing emptily.

Inside, pencils of light filtered through tiny holes in the ceiling. Everything was covered with powdery dust, but Ruthie saw enough to make her gasp in wonder. Before her lay the broken remains of a long panel composed of hundreds of pieces of disk-shaped crystalline material, each a different color from its neighbor.

When she wiped the dust away with her handkerchief, she found the colors as clear and bright as the colors of Rowen's robe.

"Where are we now?" she asked. "What are these?"

"This was the navigation area," answered Rowen, passing a hand over one of the bright disks. "This is all that remains of Jid the *querquen,* whom Tarnum killed."

Ruthie searched the panel, feeling a little bewildered. Here it was again, another unfathomable reference to Jid. "You mean this is where Jid sat. Jid was the pilot, wasn't he?"

"Jid guided the ship. Perhaps I have not explained enough. A *querquen* is not as we are. Jid's body was different. We are looking at Jid's body."

Ruthie stared at the panel again, trying to make sense of what Rowen was saying. "But this isn't a person—it's a machine, a piece of equipment."

Rowen nodded. "It is the body of a *querquen.*"

"Wait a minute," said Ruthie. "You agree that this is a machine, but you said a *querquen* was a person. That's . . . well, it's crazy. The only mechanical people I've ever heard of are robots, and they aren't really people. Anyway, this doesn't look like a robot."

"Jid was not a mechanical man . . . he was a mechanical mind," said Rowen.

"You mean, Jid was a computer?" She paused in puzzlement. "But I still don't see—how could Tarnum murder a computer? You can't murder a machine."

"The answer perhaps is that a *querquen* is far more than a computer. It is true that we Seldorians build *querquens,* as your people build computers. But a *querquen* is more. A *querquen* has a mind and emotions just as we do. It knows it exists. It is as much a person as anyone. If its body is damaged, it can die, just as anyone." Rowen brushed the dust from another of Jid's disks. "Poor Jid," he murmured.

Ruthie sat trying to imagine how magnificent Jid must have been for Rowen to be so disturbed about his destruction. Slowly, she began to understand that destroying a machine as sophisticated as Jid might not be much different from killing a human being. And she already had plenty of evidence that Tarnum would think no more of killing Rowen in cold blood than he had thought of mutilating Jid's circuitry.

Ruthie looked up in time to see Rowen groping his way through a damaged doorway. She followed him into a tangled mass of ruined equipment. There were several broken chairs from which the upholstery dangled in limp shreds. Rowen sank into one, suddenly trembling.

"What's the matter?" asked Ruthie, rushing across the cabin.

He avoided answering. Instead, he motioned her to his right. "There was a rack on this wall. It held six communicators. Perhaps it is still nearby." Pointing in the direction of another doorway, he continued, "Emergency rations were stored in there. Perhaps some are left undamaged."

"Emergency rations!" Ruthie exclaimed. "You mean the little cylinders? Like the one you used the other day?" Somehow, she had not even considered the possibility of finding additional rations in the wreckage. How could she have overlooked such an obvious chance to gain more time for Rowen?

"Yes. Like the one I used before." He sounded slightly out of breath.

Ruthie wasted no time. She dove through the doorway and began to search the cubicle that lay beyond it. In a few minutes she gave a shout of joy as she discovered a fistful of the cylinders underneath an unidentifiable mass of broken equipment.

Quickly she carried them back to Rowen who systematically examined the symbols etched into each, setting all but one aside. "Only this one contains the proper formula," he panted. "I will try it." With a click of metal on metal he placed the cylinder in the fitting on his chest, then sat back without moving until he was breathing more normally.

"It was only half full," he said when he could speak again. "Still, it will help."

"Is that it? I mean, is that the end of the rations?"

"One more half-cylinder remains in my bag."

"But you didn't tell me it was that bad. There's . . . there's practically no time left!"

"There is something that I can do. Sleep but not sleep. Make my body function more slowly. Then there is time for two sunrises more."

Two sunrises? Ruthie could hardly believe how calmly he said it.

Yet there was something in his indigo eyes that verged on desperation as he regarded her steadily. "My friend, it is not my way to ask others to do what I can do myself. But I have no wish to die. There is time for only one plan. I should now go to the camp and sleep, trusting all other things to you."

"But what'll I do, Rowen?" she responded frantically. "What if I can't find a communicator? What if I can't fix it?"

"If you desire it, I will stay awake to help you. But I will live only until morning. I trust you, my friend. You will do what is best." He said the words with a gentle

106

kindness that belied their brutal honesty. He was telling her she was his last chance for survival. He was asking for the help that she had already promised him.

"I'm sorry," said Ruthie. "Of course I'll do my best. It's just so scary." In a sudden flurry she reached for one of his hands, clasping it in her own. "I'll wake you before the second sunrise. I promise."

"How will I ever repay you?" was his only reply. Then he turned and began to find his way back into the open.

The little valley was already deep in shadow when Farmer greeted Ruthie happily at the edge of the camp. "Look what I got, boy," she said, ruffling the fur of his neck as she showed him the contents of her bandana—all six of the ship's communicators in various conditions. Farmer sniffed the bundle suspiciously.

Rowen, asleep on top of his blankets, was not able to share her triumph. Ruthie covered him gently, then set about gathering some bits of firewood. As the sun set, the temperature began to drop rapidly, and she was soon very glad for the warmth and flickering light of the small fire. She kept her rifle across her lap as she picked at an unappetizing dinner of cold canned beans. With Rowen asleep, she could not rekindle her enthusiasm for the hot meal she had planned.

Bleak as the prospect seemed, Ruthie made up her mind to keep watch all night. Wrapping herself in a blanket, she sat down with her back against a rock. But soon, her mind wandered to drowsy thoughts of home, and her eyelids drooped with weariness. Before she knew it, she had fallen fast asleep.

ELEVEN

* * * *

Voices from
Space

Late in the night, Ruthie awoke with a start. Farmer stood beside her growling. The fire had died to red, glowing embers, and she could see nothing in the thick darkness. She cocked the rifle and brought it to her shoulder, straining to catch some telltale noise that would give her a direction in which to aim. Her heart felt as if it would burst through her chest.

But long moments passed, and she heard nothing. Her arm began to ache from the weight of the rifle. The silence continued, and even Farmer grew restless. Whining, he nuzzled her. She felt the "thump, thump" of his tail as he began to relax. Finally, she released the bolt and lowered the rifle again, patting Farmer's back as she whispered, "Good boy, Farmer."

Ruthie dozed fitfully through the rest of the night, and was glad when the first rays of dawn began to brighten the eastern horizon. Numb from the chill of morning, she rebuilt the fire.

By the time she had warmed her icy hands and drunk a cup of hot coffee, the sun was up and light had begun to flood the valley. There was no sign of Tom Castor or Tarnum.

Ruthie found the stack of communicators where she'd left them the night before. Sitting down beside the fire, she began to open them one by one. Her original idea had been to try reconstructing the communicator that Tarnum had wrecked. She had brought a few tools, a box of paper clips, and a little cubical magnet for that purpose. They were now perfect for the task at hand. Each time she needed to open a case, she would rub a paper clip across the metal cube a few times. Magnetized, the clip could then be placed on the disk at the back of the case, and the intricate interior of the communicator would be exposed. Soon, all the communicators lay open before her, arranged in an orderly line like an army platoon patiently awaiting inspection.

Ruthie slowly surveyed the row. Each of the communicators differed slightly from its neighbor, and she hoped that the differences would give her enough clues to diagnose and repair one of them. She assumed that at one time they had been exactly alike and that a variation between any two of them was a sign of damage. So her first job, she decided, was to find out exactly how each communicator differed from the others. Then she might be able to figure out how an undamaged communicator was supposed to look.

The task was not easy. One by one, she picked up the devices and carefully studied the complicated arrangement of parts inside. Two of the communicators were so twisted and mangled that they were no help at all. These she placed in a separate pile. After an hour, she had only three communicators left in the line. She gazed at these until her eyes felt hot and dry. When she shut her eyes for a moment, she could still see a jumbled image of tangled wires and strange electronic components.

Eventually, Ruthie was able to choose the communicator that seemed in the best condition. Gingerly, she began to jiggle and poke at the individual parts, looking for any sign of damage. Each time she thought she detected a problem, she would compare the first communicator with the others. Then, with a few careful motions of her needle-nosed pliers, she would make sure it matched what seemed to be normal.

Rowen had shown Ruthie how the device was supposed to work. The two buttons on the outside of the case closed switches that did two different things. When one switch was closed, the communicator was a sending-and-receiving unit, something like an ordinary CB radio. The operator could speak into it and receive spoken messages in return. The other switch turned the unit into an emergency alarm and homing device.

"But aren't you worried about Earth people picking up your messages on their radios?" Ruthie had asked.

"I am told that your radios employ electromagnetic radiation. That is like the radiation that is sunlight. Our communicators use a different kind of radiation, tiny particles your scientists call neutrinos. Your radios cannot hear neutrinos, just as your ears cannot hear light."

That piece of information had really worried Ruthie, and made her feel even more lost. Basically, she had only worked on radios, and once on an old television. Rowen's communicator wasn't even a radio in any true sense, for it didn't use radio waves. All she

111

could do was apply ordinary human logic to it, and hope that her electronics background would come in handy.

After each repair, Ruthie removed the paper clip and tried the buttons, hardly knowing what to expect. When nothing happened, she would study the matter, make what changes she could with her screwdriver and pliers, then try the buttons once again. Several hours later, the sun was high in the sky, and Ruthie was sure she had opened and closed the communicator at least fifty times. Halfheartedly she pressed the buttons in quick succession. Nothing happened when she tried the first one. But when she touched the second, there was a distinct, low humming sound!

Shaking with excitement, she touched the button again. The hum returned. To Ruthie, it was the most marvelous sound she had ever heard—the sound of something happening! Laughing, she pushed the button in and out, listening as the noise came and went at her command. Then, she held the button down steadily, savoring the soft, low drone.

Without warning, *the hum gave way to a voice!* It was a strange voice that somehow reminded her of sleepy pigeons. But it was definitely a voice!

"Rowen!" she cried. "Rowen! Wake up! I think I've done it!"

It took a long time to rouse him, and even when he finally awoke, he seemed dazed. But when he understood what had happened, a smile crept across his haggard face.

"Listen," Ruthie cried excitedly. She closed the switch once more. There was the voice, loud and strong.

Ruthie held the communicator up to his mouth for him. He said something in the strange, cooing language of Seldor, then waited a moment and repeated it. He did this three times without receiving any response.

"They cannot hear me," he whispered.

Ruthie fought to control the despair that washed over her. "I'll fix it! Don't worry!" She couldn't let Rowen know how helpless she felt, or how quickly time seemed to be passing. "I'll fix it," she repeated, half to convince herself. But he didn't hear her. He had dozed off again, almost as if he were drugged.

Doggedly, Ruthie returned to the line of communicators to renew her search. Finally, half an hour later, she found one last difference among them. It was barely a noticeable difference, and one she could hardly believe was critical. But it was the only thing she could find. Attached to the tiny component board were several parts that looked like miniature strands of beads. They seemed to be made of the same crystalline material as Jid's panel, and when the sunlight fell on them they glowed brightly. But in the first communicator, one of the strands was dull and gray. It did not sparkle like the others, no matter how Ruthie held it to the light.

She could easily cut a replacement for it out of one of the other communicators. But in order to reattach it, she needed a soldering iron. She had left hers behind; it was not battery operated, and would have been useless anyway.

She tried for a long time to think of a way to make the repair without solder. But everything that occurred to her was plainly unworkable. At last, she had to admit there was only one way out. She would have to risk going back to the Bitterbrush Ranch.

When she had saddled Sundust, she tried to wake

113

Rowen again, but this time no amount of shaking worked.

"Rowen, Rowen!" she cried. "Please, wake up. There's something I have to tell you. We're so close to getting you home." But only his shallow breathing told her that he was still alive. Finally, she gently arranged his blankets and made a pillow out of her bedroll. Rowen looked so fragile and vulnerable that for a moment she decided she couldn't leave him. But in the end she knew she must.

"Please don't give up," she pleaded. "I've got to go home, but I'll be back before the second sunrise. I swear it. Just a little longer. Hang on just a little longer!"

She left him a note, scrawled in charcoal on a flat rock. She left him all the food except what she thought she would need to keep herself going. She left the

water, too, after swallowing half a cup. She poured a little into the frying pan for Farmer, who lapped it up without a second's hesitation.

Before mounting Sundust, Ruthie took Farmer's great, furry head in her hands and looked straight into his eyes. "Stay here, Farmer," she commanded. "Stay here and look after Rowen. Don't let anything happen to him."

Farmer whined and looked at her in distress as she climbed into the saddle. "Stay!" she repeated.

Whining once more, Farmer lay down beside Rowen, resting his muzzle on his front paws. Ruthie turned Sundust toward the draw in the three hills, and galloped away without looking back.

She didn't see the two shadowy figures crouched behind a rock, waiting for her to leave.

TWELVE

* * * *

Race through
the Mountains

RUTHIE pushed Sundust as hard as she dared. She knew it would be difficult—perhaps impossible—for him to gallop all the way to the Bitterbrush and back before dark, especially when he hadn't had enough feed or water the day before. But he was strong, and Ruthie knew he would give her as much of that strength as he could. She promised him a long rest in the corral, with fresh straw to lie upon, plenty of fragrant hay and cool water, and a bucket full of the finest oats. She stroked his neck as they hurtled toward the Calicos, and spoke of how she would brush him until his sleek coat shone.

Sooner than she expected, they reached the cleft in the hills where Hidden Creek sprang out of the rocks. They rested awhile there, and Ruthie filled her canteen while Sundust drank. She allowed him to graze only a minute or two, afraid he might develop colic if she pushed him hard on a belly full of grass. Then she spurred him in a flurry of dust and gravel down the western slope to the faint trail that marked the path from the ranch to the miner's shack. There, they turned south and galloped full speed toward the Bitterbrush. Luck was with her; she saw no other riders on the way. Doubtless, the searchers had already covered this territory long ago, and were off in some other part of the desert by now.

When they came within sight of the gate, Ruthie dismounted and tethered Sundust in a thick stand of cottonwoods near the little pool where one of the well pipes came up. The trees would not only keep him out of the hot afternoon sun, they would also help hide him. With two communicators shoved into her pockets, she stole toward the house, hiding in the sagebrush, her heart thudding like a bass drum.

There was no one in the yard, no one at the barn or in the garden. Ruthie crept to the side of the porch and, silent as a cat, climbed up the railing and through her bedroom window.

The room was so clean and quiet, so familiar. The spotless quilt her mother had sewn lay neatly folded on her bed. Everything was dusted, everything in its place. A cool breeze whispered in through the window, ruffling the freshly laundered white lace curtains. It was all ready, waiting for her return. She imagined her mother quietly coming up the stairs, moving about in the room, smoothing, tidying, all the while holding back tears, bravely thinking only of a happy reunion, of Ruthie's smilng return. But just in case she came home some other way . . . the room was ready for that, too. The room was waiting.

She looked in the mirror on her dresser. She was covered with dust—dust in her clothes; in her dirty, stringy hair; dust turned to mud on her cheeks where

118

tears had rolled down. She was so tired. The bed looked so good. But she thought of Rowen, and of the terrifying pace at which the sun moved down the sky. There was no time left anymore. And she had made him a promise.

Ruthie rummaged in the desk drawer until she found the soldering iron. Plugging it in, she got out the communicators and opened the cases. Carefully, she clipped out the damaged component and positioned the replacement. It took a ridiculously short time. She shook her head at the thought of having to come all this way for a job that took only five minutes. Two drops of solder were all she needed. She closed the case and tried the buttons again. This time, a steady, high-pitched beeping noise began when she punched the first button. Elated, she didn't notice what a commotion the small device was making.

Too late, she recognized the hurried sounds of someone running up the stairs. She switched the communicator off, shoved it back into her pocket, and frantically jumped for the window. But before she could get away, the bedroom door flew open and there stood her mother, wide-eyed.

"Ruthie!"

Mrs. Keag stopped, as if an invisible wall prevented her from coming closer.

Ruthie closed her eyes. She wanted to fling herself into the yard, pound down the road to Sundust and gallop away before anyone could catch her. But the look of injury on her mother's face pinned her like an arrow. She straddled the windowsill, her blood turning cold in her veins, her heart urging her to run.

"Ruthie, are you all right? Are you hurt?" Her mother took a halting step forward.

"Mom! I'll run away if you come any closer!" Ruthie cried.

Mrs. Keag stopped where she was, wringing her hands. "Ruthie, this is a mean game you're playing. For heaven's sake, stop it!"

"Just don't come any closer!" Ruthie felt like a trapped animal, no longer sure she could get away even if she had to.

Her mother's face was pale and etched with tension. "Where have you been? We've been searching all over for you. We didn't even know whether you were dead or alive."

In spite of her best efforts, a muddy tear slid down Ruthie's cheek. "Mom, I'm sorry I had to do it that way. I didn't want to—I wouldn't ever hurt you on purpose."

"You're a good girl, Ruthie. I've never doubted that. It just didn't seem that we'd ever given you a reason to run away. I know your father's harsh sometimes, but it's because he loves you. He—"

"It's got nothing to do with Dad," Ruthie broke in. "I'd have had to do it anyway. Maybe it would have been easier if he'd let me be, if he'd tried to understand." She was taken aback by the bitterness that surged inside her.

"If you're in some kind of trouble, you ought to tell us. We only want to help, you know."

Ruthie stared down at the shingles on the porch roof. "I can't tell you. There *are* reasons, and they're the best reasons in the whole universe, believe me."

"We love you! Stay home," pleaded Mrs. Keag. "We want you here."

"I know you love me," Ruthie cried raggedly. "But I can't come home yet. There's something I have to finish. Please understand. I have to go."

"Tell me what's so important! For the love of heaven, Ruthie, nothing can be *that* important."

Something in those words cut Ruthie to the bone. "I wish I could make you understand," she said softly. "This is the most important thing I'll ever do in my life. It matters more than anything else that can ever happen to me."

Mrs. Keag stood in the middle of the room, looking helpless and frightened. The breeze came through the window, carrying the scent of hay and cottonwoods.

"Mom, if you've ever trusted me before in your life, trust me now. I'll be back tomorrow. I promise."

"And you can't explain?"

"I *can* explain. But not until it's all over."

She heard Sundust whinny from the stand of trees. "I have to go now."

"They'll find you anyway, Ruthie. I couldn't stop them even if I wanted to. You know your father. He's half crazy with worry."

"I know you can't stop them. But you can give me some time. Please! Just this once."

Slowly, Mrs. Keag turned away, burying her face in her hands. "Go on!" she cried. "Go on, before I change my mind!"

Ruthie was out the window and down the roof before her mother even finished speaking. She sprinted through the gate to the cottonwoods as if the devil himself were chasing her. Her feet barely touched the stirrups as she jumped onto Sundust's back. Her mother was right. There would be no way of stopping her father. She had left a trail as easy to read as a printed page. If the searchers found out she'd been home, as they surely must, it would be an easy matter to track her across the hills and down into the little secret val-

122

ley where Rowen waited. There was just one point in her favor. It was afternoon, and there were only a few hours of light left.

By the time they reached the creek, Sundust was covered with sweat, and huffing like a steam engine. They stopped for a few minutes while he drank and caught his breath. "Just a little bit further, Sundust. Just a little further and we'll be home free." She had a few lumps of sugar in her pocket. She took them out and gave them to him. He snorted and nuzzled her for more.

"Sorry, boy. That's all. I don't have any more. But tomorrow I'll get you as many as you want." She climbed back into the saddle and they started up the hillside toward the rocky cleft where the stream gushed forth.

Then it happened. One minute they were thundering toward the crest of the hill, Sundust's shoes banging like firecrackers on the stones. The next minute, Ruthie's boots slid from the stirrups as if they'd been greased, and she felt herself flying over the horse's head.

THIRTEEN

* * * *

The Trap

Ruthie hit the ground. There was surprisingly little pain. Sprawled in the dust, she gasped and choked, fighting for air that would not come. Try as she might, she couldn't take a breath. An image of Rowen, waiting helplessly in the deserted valley, burned at the center of her consciousness. She held fast to it, knowing that if anything happened to keep her from returning, he would surely die. Just when she thought she would never breathe again, she managed a huge gulp of air. The next breath came more easily.

As she lay in the dirt with her eyes closed, she became aware of sounds. There was more than the rush of the creek alone. Someone was running. And a familiar voice was shouting her name over and over again. She felt somehow comforted by it.

She opened her eyes and sat up, feeling very dizzy. As the world slowly came into focus, she realized with a start that she was looking straight into the freckled face of Tom Castor. A wave of fear froze her. She wanted to run, and she couldn't.

But as she listened to him, her fear slowly turned to astonishment.

"I didn't mean to do it! I'm sorry!" he cried.

"What are you talking about?" she managed to gasp.

"Are you okay?" He was bending toward her, his hat clenched in his hands, his bright red hair a mass of tangles and dust.

Abruptly, everything flashed into steely clarity. The fog left her head all at once, and a second jolt of fear went through her. "Where's Sundust?" she cried. She scrambled to her feet, her boots slipping in the muddy grass at the edge of the creek.

She screamed his name aloud when she saw him. He was lying on his side. There was blood on the front of his neck. She began to run toward him.

"Stop! Stop!" shouted Tom. "There's a wire!"

Ruthie skidded to a halt not six inches from an evil-looking strand of black wire strung tightly across the trail. She turned toward Tom, her mouth agape.

"How—? Why—?" she cried incredulously.

"It was Tarnum's idea. Don't you see? I tried to take it down. . . ." His dirty face was streaked with sweat.

"Liar! You liar!" she screamed. She ducked under the wire recklessly, shouting Sundust's name time after time. He wasn't moving. He didn't make a sound.

She ran behind him and pushed on his back, half crazed with grief and rage. "Get up! Sundust, get up, boy!" she screamed. But Sundust didn't move. She wanted it to be a dream. She wanted to wake up.

"He's dead," said Tom. "Stop it, Ruthie. It won't help."

At last she could no longer deny it. "Sundust?" she whimpered. "Sundust?" And she dropped down beside him, burying her face in his still-warm flank.

"Ruthie?" said Tom softly. He touched her shoulder. "I was on my way to warn you."

Disgust welled up within Ruthie. She sobbed into Sundust's sweat-dulled coat; suddenly, the horrors of the past few days overwhelmed her. It wasn't Tarnum alone who had caused Pearl to throw Kate, and she wouldn't believe it was Tarnum alone who had killed Sundust!

With a shriek of rage, she leaped to her feet, spun around and delivered a double-fisted blow to Tom's stomach. Tom, caught by surprise, doubled over with pain. Ruthie flung herself at him, pummeling his head and face. He held up one arm to fend off the rain of punches, but made no attempt to return the blows.

All at once, Ruthie stopped, staggering back a step. She was suddenly dizzy again; there was a sharp pain in her shoulder that she hadn't noticed before.

"I don't feel very good," she mumbled. The air seemed to be filled with dark, flying creatures. There were more and more of them, until finally she couldn't see anything at all.

When the dark things disappeared, she found herself lying face-up in the mud. Tom was bent over her, pressing something cold and wet to her forehead.

"Come on, Ruthie. Let me take you into town. You need a doctor."

"I'm okay," she snapped, pushing away the wet bandana he held to her face.

"You are not. Your shoulder's all torn up. I wouldn't be surprised if it was broken."

She sat up and reached around, touching the painful shoulder experimentally.

"But I *can't* go to town. Not now!" she cried. "I have to get back to Rowen."

Tom shook his head and looked away. "I don't think

there's much help for him," he said in a low voice. "Tarnum's still back at the ship."

"You mean Tarnum is back there alone with Rowen?" she cried in disbelief. "But Rowen's helpless! Tarnum'll kill him. Tom, I've got to get back to the ship, right now. As fast as I can."

"You're crazy," Tom replied. "You need a doctor right away. Come on. I can take you to Sand Fork on my motorcycle."

Ruthie wanted to scream, to blot out the specter of failure. If she couldn't save Rowen now, it was all for nothing. Sundust was dead, and soon Rowen would be, too. How could she face such a cruel and empty world?

In her anger and pain, Ruthie lashed out at Tom. "I always thought you'd grow up to be better than that stinking, drunken father of yours. But I guess I was wrong! You're even worse," she shouted.

Tom looked at her as if she'd slapped him. His teeth were clenched, and she could see that he was straining to hold back tears. "Take it back!" he cried.

"Do something right for once in your life. Take me to the ship!" Ruthie retorted.

Tom glared at her bitterly. "You need a doctor. That's what's right. Only you're too dumb to see it."

"Rowen's going to die. And if he does, it will be all your fault!"

Tom's cheeks were red with anger. For a moment, he didn't move. Then, slowly, he started toward the motorcycle. "Come on, then. If that's what you want, I'll take you there."

In a haze of pain, Ruthie retrieved her saddlebags and her rifle from Sundust's lifeless body. "Good-bye, boy," she whispered. Then, determined not to look back, she climbed up behind Tom on the noisy motorcyle.

128

FOURTEEN

* * * *

Found

RUTHIE was only dimly aware of the dodging, twisting path Tom took down the hillside. She closed her eyes, concentrating everything she had on just holding tight. It seemed like hours before they were down on the flats at last, rushing toward the Dutchman's Ladies in the near distance. Just when she wondered how much longer she could hold on, they smoked through the entrance to the little valley.

Tom headed directly into the camp, where they were greeted by Farmer, who barked savagely, ready to defend Rowen to the death. He refused to let Tom off the motorcycle until Ruthie spoke reassuringly and allowed him to sniff Tom's hand. Still suspicious, Farmer at last gave in.

Just then, Ruthie caught sight of something moving on the opposite hillside. "Look!" she cried, pointing. In the fading light, they could just make out Tarnum, struggling away through the sagebrush as if his life depended on it.

An icicle of fear caught Ruthie on its tip. "Rowen!" she cried. "Are you okay?" And with all her remaining willpower she made her way across the rocky clearing to where Rowen lay motionless, wrapped in blankets just as she had left him that morning.

His eyes were open wide. He gazed up at her. "I am not harmed," he murmured. "Farmer took good care of me. I am glad that you came back."

"Yes, yes, I'm back," she grinned in immense relief. "And listen." Fumbling in her pocket, she held the communicator up for him. The emergency signal pulsed steadily. She took one of his cold, thin hands. "They'll hear it. Now they'll come."

He didn't speak. But joy and hope transformed his face for a moment before he closed his eyes once more, dropping back into his deep sleep.

Later that night, she sat with Tom beside the tall, dancing campfire. Sleep was impossible. Anxiety over Rowen's rescue made her feel as tight as a piano wire in spite of her exhaustion. The pain in her shoulder had become a steady, grinding throb. This in itself would have kept her awake. But she almost welcomed it; it helped keep her mind off the greater pain of Sundust.

"We must have scared Tarnum off," she said, thinking aloud. "I'm sure glad I left Farmer here."

"Yeah," said Tom, absently scratching doodles in the ground with a broken stick. "It was probably the best move you could have made. He's scared of that dog—more than ever after he got bit night before last."

"Farmer bit him? Then it *was* you and Tarnum prowling around our camp!"

"Yeah," said Tom curtly, avoiding her eyes.

After a long pause, he added, "Tarnum won't get far. He's sick, real sick—like the old man there."

"I know," said Ruthie. The discord between them almost crackled in the air. Tom shifted uncomfortably.

130

Taking a deep breath, Ruthie offered, "Look, I'm sorry I said that about your father."

"Well, you were right," he replied sullenly, still refusing to look up.

"That doesn't matter. I shouldn't have said it."

There was another long, awkward pause. Then Tom burst out, "I didn't mean to hurt you. I would have ripped that wire down if I had gotten there in time. I tried!"

Ruthie couldn't answer. The memory was still too much to bear. She had tried to force it out of her mind, to concentrate on the tasks still at hand.

"Tarnum put it up!" Tom insisted, gazing at her imploringly. "It's not just wire. It's some kind of stuff he got from the wreck. It's practically indestructible." He flung the stick into the fire. "I didn't know what he was like when I first took him in. He promised things. He promised he'd take me away with him, to places I couldn't even dream of . . . make me *somebody*. You know what that meant to me? You think I want to spend my life in this raggedy little town, tryin' to make up for my parents' mistakes?" There were tears in Tom's eyes. "He asked me to *do* things—things I knew were wrong. And I did them. Because I wanted him to take me away. I wanted it bad enough to do anything he told me to."

Ruthie would have said something, anything, but she couldn't. No words would come.

"I always liked you and your folks, Ruthie. You're the only real family I've ever had. I didn't mean to hurt you, I swear."

"Never mind," she replied, finding her tongue at last. "I knew Tarnum must have been behind it. It wasn't like you." She swallowed a lump in her throat as she thought of Sundust, lying alone in the chilly

darkness by the creek. Then she couldn't go on, though she'd meant to soothe Tom further.

Ruthie stared up at the clear, moonless sky. There was nothing in it but stars. What if the Seldorians never came? What if the communicator was sending no signal, just giving off falsely reassuring sounds? She couldn't bear to think of that either.

She listened to the thunk of wood on wood and the sharp crackling of hot sap as Tom threw more branches on the fire. After a moment, she struggled awkwardly to her feet. She achieved an unsteady balance, then walked slowly to where Rowen lay. Renewed pain seared her shoulder as she knelt beside him. His sleep was so deep, so motionless, that she had to lean close to feel him breathing. There was no color left in his thin, withered face. Briefly she wondered again what Tarnum had stolen. What human artifact could possibly have been worth all this?

"Ruthie!" Tom's shout wrenched her away from her reverie. "Ruthie, look! They're coming!"

Tom was pointing toward the entrance to the valley, where the barren hills were illuminated by a vague, yellow glow. But with the glow came the faint whine of engines and, soon after, great, billowing clouds of dust.

"No!" Ruthie cried. "No! Not the search party!"

Roused by the sudden commotion, Rowen whispered, "Has the ship arrived? Have they come?"

Ruthie didn't answer. Her attention was riveted on the steadily increasing roar in the distance. The yellow glow had condensed into five pairs of bouncing headlights that were now aimed straight at the small encampment. It was too late to run, too late to hide.

As if by silent command, the headlights suddenly spread out, and soon Rowen, Tom, and Ruthie were encircled by three jeeps and two pickup trucks. Ruthie recognized her father's jeep and saw from the official markings on another that Sheriff Thompson was there as well. One by one, the engines sputtered into silence; doors swung open and men began to clamber out.

"Ruthie! Are you all right?" It was her father's voice, hoarse with worry and fatigue. "Did he hurt you? Why, if he did, I'll . . ." Mr. Keag's angry gaze was fixed beyond her, on Rowen.

Confused, Ruthie looked around the rapidly forming circle of men. Steve Washoe, Mr. Sheldon, and many other residents of Sand Fork stood among them.

133

Several of them had guns, and all of the guns were pointed directly at Rowen. It was as if he were a criminal and the searchers expected him to leap up and run off into the desert.

"Dad, I'm okay," Ruthie cried. "I don't know what you're talking about. Rowen's my friend."

Sheriff Thompson stepped forward from the grim circle. His uniform was covered with dirt, and sweat stains formed dark, symmetrical patterns on his shirt. Ruthie noticed that the desert grime did not seem to affect the aura of strength and authority that perpetually surrounded the sheriff. She had always liked Sheriff Thompson, but now his serious manner unnerved her.

Ignoring Ruthie, the sheriff strode quickly to where Rowen lay. Towering above the motionless figure, he said in an even, matter-of-fact tone, "Mister, you're under arrest for kidnapping this girl and for killing her horse."

Ruthie could not believe her ears. Searching wildly through the faces around her, she found the answer to her unspoken questions. Between two of the sheriff's deputies, slightly behind the rest of the men, stood Tarnum, grinning with self-satisfaction.

FIFTEEN

* * * *

The Promise

RUTHIE stared at Tarnum until his leering face seemed to dominate the entire scene before her. Couldn't the others see it? Couldn't they see the mocking expression, the contempt he radiated? Instead, they glared at Rowen, as if Tarnum's dizzying influence had taken away their ability to tell up from down, good from bad. She felt a sickening, cold emptiness creep over her, devouring her strength as relentlessly as a locust devours a green leaf.

"*He* told you that story, didn't he?" Ruthie finally cried, pointing accusingly at Tarnum. Her outstretched arm trembled like a sapling in a windstorm. She could hardly speak; her tongue felt thick and cottony.

"Well, he's lying!" She wanted to scream, to laugh, to cry. She wanted to break the spell that hung over the solemn group of men. "He's the one who killed Sundust. And he's been trying to kill Rowen, too. *He's* the one who spooked Kate's horse. He's lying to save his own skin."

A brief murmur arose from the circle of men. Soon all eyes were turned expectantly toward Sheriff Thompson, and the crackling fire was once again the only sound.

The sheriff's hand moved quietly to rest on the open flap of his black leather holster. When he spoke, the words came slowly and deliberately.

"I don't know what's going on," he began, "but it's something mighty strange." Pausing, he looked from Rowen over to Tarnum, then back down at Rowen again.

"The way I see it, there's only one thing I can do," he continued. "I'm placing you both under arrest, and when we get back to Sand Fork, I want to hear both of your stories."

"You can't do that!" Ruthie's voice was almost a scream. "If you take Rowen to Sand Fork, he'll die!"

Ruthie's father shook his head. "Ruth, don't talk that way to the sheriff. You know as well as I do that there are doctors in Sand Fork."

"The doctor can't help Rowen," Ruthie pleaded, turning to face her father. "You've got to leave us here."

Standing next to Mr. Keag, Steve Washoe averted his eyes in embarrassment. She realized that even Steve thought she had gone crazy. Suddenly, she felt very tired, very alone. The pain in her shoulder surged like a fountain of fire.

"Sheriff Thompson." It was Tom Castor's voice, reedy with tension. "Ruthie's right. If you're gonna arrest anybody, it should be me and Tarnum. Tarnum did all that stuff, and I helped him do it. If you want proof, look at him. He's wearing the clothes I stole for him from the general store."

In the flickering light on the other side of the camp-fire, Tarnum's face distorted with fury. "Fool! You are a fool!" he shrieked.

Before the men could move to stop him, Tarnum lunged forward in one continuous, fluid motion. By the time Ruthie realized what was happening, the alien had tackled Tom like a player in some unbelievable football game. The jarring impact sent a fine spray of desert sand into the fire, which recoiled like a startled animal.

The scuffle was over as quickly as it had begun. In two huge strides, Steve Washoe reached the pair. Firmly and effortlessly he lifted Tarnum high in the air and held him suspended in a powerful grasp. "I'd say *you* are the fool," Steve thundered.

Sheriff Thompson deftly snapped handcuffs on Tarnum as Steve eased him gently to the ground. "Well, I guess we know who to listen to now," the sheriff said, turning toward Ruthie. "I hope you're ready to explain exactly what's—" In mid-sentence, Sheriff Thompson's voice trailed off, though his mouth continued in a silent pantomime. His eyes were fixed somewhere above Ruthie's head. "What the devil is *that?*" he murmured.

The tone of his voice made the hair on Ruthie's neck stand on end. Spinning around, she looked out across the starlit valley. There was something on the hill, something luminous and gigantic, like a huge moon rising over the ridge.

"Rowen! Rowen! They're here!" Ruthie shouted.

Reaching toward the great ball of light with trembling arms, Rowen cried out, "My friend, we have won! They have arrived!"

As the immense, radiant sphere maneuvered its way over the hills and down into the valley, strange

gusts of hot wind sprang up from all directions. Blown sand and twigs swirled around them. A deep, bone-jarring hum filled the air. From somewhere in the shadows, Farmer began a high-pitched keening of fright. Soon the phosphorescent craft hovered like thistledown above the scattered wreckage that was once Rowen's ship. A slender ramp began to drop down from its rounded belly as the wind died away, leaving only the faint smell of lightning.

The men from Sand Fork cowered, running for cover wherever they could find it. Sheriff Thompson pulled Tarnum behind a large, jagged boulder. Only Tom, Rowen, and Ruthie remained in the open, bathed in the ship's eerie light.

"Ruthie! Get out of there!" Mr. Keag's voice seemed to come from far away. "Tom, get her away!"

"It's okay, Dad. Don't worry," Ruthie said as she began to walk slowly toward the still-descending ramp. She was filled with an exultation deeper than anything she'd ever known before.

Hushed whispers briefly arose from the shadows behind the boulders. But when Ruthie reached the base of the ramp, now firmly settled on the desert floor, the whispers gave way to an expectant silence.

The silence was answered by a quiet but penetrating voice. "This is a mission of goodwill. We have been summoned by a signal of distress. We hoped to find our friends." Its warm resonance made Ruthie wonder if the voice belonged to a woman.

"I sent the signal," Ruthie said, searching for the source of the voice. But when she found nothing, she directed her response toward the empty ramp. "I sent it for Rowen, who is lying back there. He needs medical help—emergency rations right away."

139

Behind her, Rowen began speaking. His voice was hardly more than a thick whisper, but by now Ruthie easily recognized the odd, lilting tones of the Seldorian language. The ship returned a songlike message of its own, and Rowen replied with a long succession of cooing sounds.

At last, the voice once again spoke in English. "Ruthie Keag, we are greatly in debt for all you have done," it said. Ruthie stared nervously down at the sand, unable to reply. The voice continued. "But now we must ask of you one additional favor."

"I . . . I'll try." Her response sounded thin and wispy after the reverberant voice from the ship.

"We ask that you accompany our emissary, to speak to those who hold Tarnum."

"Sure," Ruthie answered, looking up the long, smooth ramp. At the top were three unmoving figures, silhouetted in the bright light of the ship's interior. She wondered how long they had stood there, watching her from above. She had noticed no motion, heard no sounds. But she knew they hadn't been there a moment before.

The figures began walking down the ramp. They were clad in brightly colored robes like Rowen's, though the pattern of the splendid hues was noticeably different. It was not until they had descended beneath the glare that Ruthie could finally discern their smooth, Seldorian features. Two of them were men, but the third figure was smaller and sleeker. It was a Seldorian woman, somewhat older than her companions. Fascinated, Ruthie watched their approach. They walked slowly, stopping now and then to look around them or to gaze into the darkness at the bottom of the ramp. The youngest man, walking to the woman's left, carried a small box.

"Ruthie Keag? My name is Metlan," the woman said. Her smile was soft and almost shy. Could this be the first time she had ever seen a human, Ruthie wondered in surprise? "With your permission, we wish to care for Rowen," said Metlan, bowing quickly.

The two men also bowed as they passed Ruthie hurridly, and one said a few words in Seldorian. Then they strode rapidly to Rowen's side and began busily taking objects out of the box. Beyond them, Ruthie saw the men from Sand Fork poking their heads out from behind their basalt shields, wide-eyed in amazement.

"Are you the person who's been talking from the ship?" Ruthie asked, turning back to Metlan.

The woman's eyes twinkled and she laughed softly, then smiled as if Ruthie had made a delightful joke. "No, that is Gwel," she replied. "Gwel must remain aboard the ship."

"Gwel . . ." Ruthie paused, recalling the resonant voice that sounded so warm, so alive. "Gwel must be a *querquen!*"

"I see you have learned much about Seldor," Metlan said, smiling again.

Ruthie grinned back. "It's all thanks to Rowen," she said.

It was half an hour before the Seldorians began packing their equipment back into the box. By that time, Rowen was sitting upright, and already seemed like his old self. Even so, his friends wouldn't let him stand up; no doubt the excitement made him feel better than he really was, and the Seldorians wanted to take no chances.

The time had passed quickly for Ruthie. Once her father and Sheriff Thompson had come out from behind the rocks, the rest of the search party cautiously joined them. Ruthie easily persuaded the sheriff to turn Tarnum over to the Seldorians; in fact, he had seemed more than glad to get rid of the criminal. After that, the time was spent answering questions. The men wanted to hear all the details of Ruthie's story. All of them had questions about Seldor. Metlan answered the questions, sometimes asking Ruthie for help, sometimes asking strange, careful questions of her own. Ruthie was quickly convinced that Metlan was as amazed by the humans as they were by the Seldorians.

While one of the Seldorians finished repacking their medical equipment, the other came over and spoke briefly with Metlan. Turning to Ruthie, the woman said softly, "It is nearly time for us to leave. Rowen has asked to speak to you before we go."

Ruthie walked to where Rowen sat propped against a smooth boulder.

"Feeling better?" she asked, smiling.

"Thanks only to you, my friend," Rowen answered, with a sparkle in his eyes.

"So, I guess you're going now?"

"Yes. But first I have a small gift for you."

He reached into a gilded box that lay beside him on his blanket. From it he took two faintly glowing crystal spheres about the size of hen's eggs. He held them up before her.

"From the rings of Rhō Cygni, the dwarf star. These are *terweni,* the globes of healing. One is for you and one for your friend who was injured by Tarnum. Keep the *terweni* nearby. In a day or two days your shoulder will be much improved. A gift too small to repay such a debt." Rowen tucked the glassy spheres carefully into her hand. "I regret that we cannot help Sundust also. Though we travel among stars, we have no power over death."

Ruthie gazed mutely at his firelit face, unable to reply. Softly, the great ship had again begun to hum.

"Time passes, my friend. But before we go, tell me. Is there some other thing we can do for you?"

Ruthie shrugged stiffly, unable at first to think of anything. Then, slowly, she said, "Can I ask a question? What was it that Tarnum stole? What started it all?"

"Ah," said Rowen, reaching for his bag. Carefully, he drew something flat and heavy from it. "Just this," he said quietly, and laid the object on her lap.

It was a metal plaque. Ruthie read the inscription aloud.

HERE MEN FROM PLANET EARTH
FIRST SET FOOT UPON THE MOON.
JULY 1969 A.D.
WE CAME IN PEACE FOR ALL MANKIND.

"My gosh!" she whispered. "No wonder it was so important." She handed it back to him as if it were made of eggshell.

"Before we return to Seldor, we will replace it. All will be as before," said Rowen.

"Almost," Ruthie answered. Someday an explorer from Earth might pay a visit to that first landing site. And there he would find footprints unlike the others— small, inexplicable. And only she, Ruthie Keag, would know to whom they belonged.

"I'll miss you, Rowen! I'll miss you so much!" she

cried suddenly, throwing her arms around him, hugging him as a flood of tears coursed down her cheeks.

"I will tell Leral all the things about you," he said in the moondusty voice so familiar to her now. "Together we will speak of you often."

By now, the hum of the ship had become a deep roar that could be felt as well as heard. Two of the Seldorians returned to Rowen's side and spoke rapidly in the strange tongue, their voices raised against the increasing onslaught of sound.

"My friend," said Rowen as they helped him to his feet, "let us make to one another a promise."

"Anything—anything at all," she replied.

"I will return. One day we will meet again, here in this desert valley. And if you wish it then, I will take you away to see Seldor. I give you my word."

"I'll be here—I promise!" The Seldorians supporting Rowen turned and began walking him toward the ramp. "But when? How will I know?"

"I will send you a sign," he cried above the noise of the ship. They had reached the bottom of the ramp, where Metlan stood waiting, her hands folded tightly. "I promise, my friend," were the last words Ruthie heard him say.

As they disappeared into the craft, the voice of Gwel the *querquen* pierced the deafening rumble. "Please go up into the hills." Though it could easily be heard, the voice showed no sign of strain; it was not a shout. "We have business to finish and do not wish to harm you."

Mr. Keag gathered Ruthie in his strong, warm arms, and he and Tom helped her struggle up over the rocks and through the brush. Not until the valley floor lay well below them did they stop and look back. By

then, the Seldorian ship floated far above the valley and the hills where they stood.

As they watched, a long, blue tongue of fire leaped from the belly of the ship to the desert below. When the air cleared, the wreck of Rowen's craft was gone; in its place was a smoking crater.

Then the ship streaked silently away to the northwest at a speed Ruthie would not have dreamed was possible. Over the distant Calico Hills, they saw another stream of fire, and felt the distant rumble of an explosion.

"That must have been the miner's shack," whispered Tom. "I guess they didn't want to leave anything there, either."

Later, Ruthie lay in a soft quilt in the back of her father's jeep as they jostled toward home. The muffled sound of voices filtered back from the men in front, accenting the uneven drone of the engine. Ruthie opened her eyes and looked up into the southern sky, searching for Antares and its two bright companions. "Goodbye, Rowen," she murmured sleepily. "I'll be waiting."

EPILOGUE

* * * *

THE old wicker porch chair creaked as Kate leaned forward to adjust the lightweight sling around her shoulder. It was almost dusk, and the desert surrounding the Bitterbrush Ranch was already awash with long purple shadows.

"Boy, what a dinner!" Kate breathed. "Almost like Thanksgiving."

Ruthie smiled. "Well, we wanted it to be a real celebration," she replied. "Wait'll you taste Mom's homemade peach ice cream. Hope you saved plenty of room."

"Ruthie, if you only knew how awful that hospital food was, you'd see what a perfect celebration this really is." Kate patted her stomach happily.

"It's good to have you back."

"Well, if it weren't for you, I'd have spent a lot more than three days in that place," said Kate, shaking her head.

"No, not me," Ruthie replied softly. The *terweni* had worked just as Rowen said they would. Kate's arm was almost completely healed, and the pain in Ruthie's shoulder had long since disappeared without a trace.

In the house, Ruthie's father whistled cheerfully as he banged about, helping her mother fill the ice-cream maker. The fragrance of fresh peaches and sugar wafted out onto the porch. It all seemed so ordinary, so humdrum. Ruthie squeezed the *terweni* in her pocket and tried to imagine the rings of Rhō Cygni. She thought of the star-drenched highways of space, and she longed to be there.

Her reverie was broken by the squeak of the screen door as Mr. Keag stepped out onto the porch carrying the heavy ice-cream bucket. Mrs. Keag followed with a tray of dishes and spoons.

"I'll help, Dad," Ruthie offered, glad to think of other things. She scrambled out of her chair and sat down beside the ice-cream maker. Grabbing the handle, she began turning it.

For a few minutes, they sat in easy silence as the twilight deepened. Crickets began a melodious harmony with the creak of the turning handle. Soon the comfortable scent of Mr. Keag's hand-rolled cigarette drifted across the evening air.

"Say, what's that?" Kate asked abruptly, pointing down the road toward the gate.

"Looks like a pickup truck," said Mr. Keag, without the least hint of surprise in his voice. "Seems to be pulling a horse trailer."

"A horse trailer?" Ruthie looked up from the ice-cream maker. She stood slowly and moved to the front of the porch, trying to get a better view of the unfamiliar truck. She squinted to see if she could identify the person behind the wheel. "I wonder who it could be?"

The truck pulled up in a cloud of dust and the driver jumped out immediately. "Uh, hi, Ruthie," he said, removing his hat with a grin.

It was Tom Castor, looking cleaner and more carefully dressed than she'd ever seen him before. He wore a freshly ironed Western shirt with a string tie and a new pair of blue jeans. His usually tangled red curls had been brushed into submission with plenty of water and hair tonic.

Ruthie was so surprised she forgot to return his greeting.

"I've . . . I've, uh, got something for you," said Tom, fidgeting with his hatband. "Wanna see it?"

"Sure," said Ruthie, finding her tongue at last. She walked down the porch steps, holding the old wooden railing to keep her hand from shaking.

Stepping to the back of the trailer, Tom opened the doors and put down the ramp. A moment later, he stood before Ruthie, leading the most beautiful colt she had ever seen.

Ruthie reached out to touch the silky mane. "He's . . . he's terrific," she stammered.

"He's yours," said Tom, handing her the lead.

"Oh, Tom!" Ruthie whispered.

"I bought him from Gus over at the Lazy B," said Tom proudly. "He's one of Sundust's grandsons."

"Thank you, Tom," was all she could say.

Stars were winking to life in the dark heavens, and the palomino colt stood etched against them in shining perfection. It was as if, in some mysterious fashion, Sundust had found his way back to her.

The constellations wheeled above them as they led the colt toward the barn. Tom looked across at her, his cheeks burning in the darkness. "When Rowen comes back, do you think he'd take me, too?" he asked softly.

"Of course he will," Ruthie answered, linking her arm through his.

Poor Little Cigarette—
she had no home but the streets

FLIGHT OF THE SPARROW

BY JULIA CUNNINGHAM

author of *Dorp Dead*

When Mago found her, she was in the furnace room of the orphanage. He gave her a name—Little Cigarette—and brought her to his home, the streets of Paris. For Cigarette, it was almost like having a real family—and Mago gave her the courage to survive.

But survival sometimes means having to hurt those you care most about. And when Cigarette is forced to steal a valuable painting from an artist friend, she must flee Paris. Armed only with love, she begins a frightening and extraordinary journey to try to make things right. Maybe she can earn a chance at happiness that Mago and the other street people never had.

"Exciting and poignant."—School Library Journal*

AN AVON CAMELOT ● 57653-8 ● $1.95

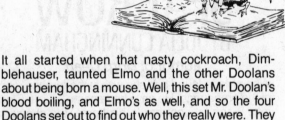

"A beautifully wrought story of a mountain Mary Poppins."—
School Library Journal

IDA EARLY COMES OVER THE MOUNTAIN

by Robert Burch
(author of *Queenie Peavie*)

Life was rough in the Blue Ridge Mountains of Georgia, but things certainly took a turn for the lively when Ida Early came over the mountain! For the four Sutton children, Ida appeared just in time. With their mother dead, their father at work, and unpredictable Ida hired on as housekeeper, bossy Aunt Earnestine might finally go back to Atlanta.

Ida brought laughter back into the household. And the Suttons grew to love the tall tales she told at the toss of her hat. But their friendship was put to the test when the Sutton kids learned that there was more to Ida Early than just her funny ways.

An ALA Notable Book
AN AVON CAMELOT ● 57091-2 ● $1.95